RESOLUTIONS

THE PUNISHER

--- PULLING THREADS ---

Book Nine

SHERYLL O'BRIEN

This is a work of fiction. All characters in this book are the product of an overactive imagination. Any businesses, organizations, places, events, and incidents are used fictionally. Any resemblance to a real person, living or dead, is a tremendous coincidence.

WOODWIND PRESS

Printed in United States of America

Mom,

I love your threat ---
"I don't care who you kill off,
but it better never be, Malcolm!"

ACKNOWLEDGMENT

To my English teachers –
sure do wish you had spent more time teaching me
when **not** to use commas!

A heartfelt thank you to my team:

Andria Flores ~ Editor extraordinaire.
Nancy Pendleton ~ Goddess of the publishing world.
Jessica Champion ~ Web designer and manager.
25 Hours Consulting
Daryl Bruinsma ~ Cover Design & Animation.

Testimonials

"One book will set the hook!" ~ Nancy Pendleton

"This avid reader predicts that Sheryll O'Brien will become your favorite author. She's mine." ~ Ruth S. Bodreau

"The characters draw you in immediately. You will worry, laugh, hope, and love right along with them." ~ Donna Eaton

"There is nothing sweeter than a Sunday morning coffee, a blanket, overcast skies, and a *Pulling Threads* novel." ~ Andria Flores

"Everything you'd want in a good book. Humor, romance, suspense and great characters! It even takes place by the ocean! Loved it." ~ Helena Green

"I could write a book about the wonderfulness of it all." ~ Faith Lavallee

"Hunks, humor, and heartache! What more could you ask for?" ~ Marjorie McCarthy

"*Bullet Bungalow* is a page turning family saga and then *Netti Barn* and *Cutters Cove* come along and add a whole lot of trauma to the drama." ~ Jessica O'Brien

"The most promising new author I've encountered in my publishing career!" ~ Jim P. - Woodwind Press

--- Pulling Threads ---

Bullet Bungalow
Netti Barn
Cutters Cove
They Run
They Hide
They Choose

PENOBSCOT BAY
A Rocco Fiancetti Incorporated Investigation

Reasons
Rescues
Resolutions

Coming soon…

Torment
Tango
Tests
Resolve
Revenge
Rebound

--- Twisted Threads ---

Coming soon…

Her Scream
Stay Safe

Thirty-five thousand feet in the air.

"Penny for your thoughts." Gretchen Mitchell whispers, then shoulder-nudges her travel companion, Malcolm Price. "You've been awfully quiet. Are you alright? Is it Damian? Do you want to go back to Lewisburg?"

The MAN with a broadening smile takes his woman's hand and kisses her knuckles, "Yes, I'm alright. Yes, I'm concerned about Damian. Yes, I want to go back to Lewisburg, but it's important we take this time away." He follows the path of his woman's cornflower blue eyes. They land on two people who've just begun their journey in life — Manuel Xavier and the sweet little wonder born that afternoon at 3:33 PM, his daughter, Charlotte. "That's a sight," Malcolm smiles wide.

Gretchen silences a laugh when she sees the look on Manuel's face. "You okay, over there?"

"Do I look okay?"

"Nope. Nope. You look terrified, which is somewhat surprising considering you are…"

"A former Federal agent who infiltrated a criminal organization in Peru, kidnapped a kidnapped victim, pissed off a worldwide syndicate, hid out for months, and outlived a bounty."

"Yes – all that. How is it possible you did all that, yet an itty-bitty baby has rendered you an unglued mess?"

"Haven't a clue." He looks at Charlotte, then looks back at Gretchen, "She's been asleep for hours. Are they supposed to sleep for hours?"

Gretchen laughs, "I don't know. The discharge nurse at the penitentiary said," Gretchen stalls, "well, **that** sure sounded strange. Anyway, the discharge nurse did a top to bottom exam, and the escort nurse fed and changed her before we boarded the jet, so I suspect all is well with Charlotte."

"I need her to sleep until we land."

"Then what?"

"I don't know. I'm hoping someone at The Compound will tell me what to do. Jesus, Gretchen. This kid needs a mother and a father. I am neither of those things."

"Well, that isn't entirely true, Manuel. You are one of those two things." She looks to Malcolm for some help. Nudges him when none is offered.

"What?"

"Say something."

"What?"

"I don't know. Say something reassuring."

"It's been five hours and she's still alive."

Manuel places his palm onto Charlotte's tiny head and whispers,

"Good God, it's only been five hours?"

Resolutions

Sit your butt on that seat.

The jet lands somewhere. It taxis away from the airport terminal and down a dimly lit runway. It comes to a stop, powers down, and waits. Lights from two transport vehicles shine from just beyond a cyclone fence. A gated section swings open and the two vehicles inch forward coming to a stop just beyond the nose of the jet. A very pregnant, Maura Putnam, steps out and boards the jet, sort of waves to the occupants inside, and gets to work. "You need to move, Manuel."

Relief floods his face.

"Don't go far," she instructs, then unbuckles the newborn from her car seat and lifts her with a soothing coo, "Well hello, Miss Charlotte." Maura is rewarded with a wail. "Oh, I know. This is all so new. I just need to take a peek-see then we'll get you fed and to your new home." A quick unsnap of her onesie, a change of her diaper, a chest check with a stethoscope, the donning of her outfit, and the adding of a bib and matching smiley-face hat, and the baby is ready for a bottle. "Sit," she instructs Manuel.

"Why?"

"You're going to feed her."

"I am not."

"Sit your butt on that seat."

He sits.

Gretchen laughs from across the aisle.

He scowls then follows Maura's pantomime – he bends his elbow and puts his arm tight against his torso. Maura places Charlotte's head into the crook of Manuel's elbow, nestles the baby's chest against his chest and positions her back along his arm, her tiny feet end at his hand. He touches one, "Tiny." Charlotte starts squirming, turning her head from one side to the other.

"She's hungry." Maura hands Manuel a bottle. "I've checked it, and it's perfectly fine, but I want you to get used to checking the temperature of the formula. You need to do this every time **before** you put the nipple into her mouth. Turn your wrist over and let a few drops hit your skin. You shouldn't feel any significant temperature – not hot, not cold."

He tests the formula and reports, "Barely warm."

Maura smiles and touches Manuel's shoulder. "You're good to go. Just put the nipple to her lips, she'll do the rest."

He does his part. She does the rest – then she stops.

Manuel inspects the bottle, "There's still some left."

"But she's done. She's the boss, Manuel, so learn to read her cues, and follow her lead." Maura reaches out, "Hand her to me. Make sure you support her head and neck while I scoop her. Okay, now move over." He removes the car seat and hands it off to Gretchen, who has become spectator #1. Manuel sits. Maura sits. "The baby needs to be burped after every feeding. **Every** feeding, Manuel. She needs to expel the air she pulled in with her formula, if you don't help her get there, she will be in distress, and she will let you know."

"How?"

"Oh good Lord. She'll sent you a registered letter," Maura scoffs. Gretchen laughs.

Maura continues, "She'll cry. Really, really loud!"

"Right. Of course," he stammers.

"Oh good Lord," she scoffs again. "There are several methods of burping, two of them are recommended for a newborn." Maura places a burp diaper onto her shoulder. "This is the most used method." She puts Charlotte up onto her shoulder and does the whole back-tap-rubbing thing. "It's tried and true. The other method works really well for some babies because there's a bit more pressure applied to the belly which forces the air bubble up and out." Maura sets Charlotte onto her knee, puts her hand under the infant's chin, and tilts the baby forward. Maura hasn't even started the whole back-tap-rubbing thing when Charlotte lets out a wonderful burp.

Manuel beams, "She did it. Wow."

Maura and Gretchen crack up.

"What?"

"Nothing," they say in unison.

"Okay, let's roll." Maura carries the newborn to the transport vehicle, straps her into an infant car seat, points to the seat next to the babe, and says, "Get in." When the new father is buckled in, she hands him a pink baby blanket, and a pacifier in the shape of cartoon lips. With a pat on the shoulder, she says, "Charlotte is beautiful. Good luck, Daddy." She climbs into the front seat, pulls her door closed, and laughs—big! "Manuel Xavier, a father, well that just about beats all," she laughs harder.

"I thought my father sidelined you," Manuel growls.

"Not even the almighty Rocco Fiancetti could keep me from participating in this momentous occasion," she laughs.

Mr. Mom

The arriving travelers have very different reasons for making the trip to the secret fortress; father and daughter will begin family life at the heavily guarded Rocco Fiancetti Compound; Gretchen Mitchell will be celebrated for her personal and professional victories over Antonio Alvarez and Cappa Escobar; and Malcolm Price will be honoring a debt. In a sort-of quid pro quo agreement, the basketball legend agreed play a little b-ball with Callie and Tess, the sort-of daughters of RFI associate Fred Serpico in lieu of paying RFI for services rendered in the Cappa Escobar *catch or kill* plan. That is the **supposed** reason why Malcolm Price is traveling to an international crime busting compound in the middle of nowhere. The **real** reason for his trip — he needs the services of that international crime busting team.

When the visiting group steps from their transport vehicles they are met by a rag-tag group of gun-toting, cyber-hunting, karate-chopping, secret-snooping, criminal-catching men and women. After an abundance of oohing and aahing over the newborn, the RFI team heads indoors, sans Fred Serpico, who remains outside.

"Why are you still here, Fred?" the new father asks.

"Because Charlotte is here."

"Oh fuck, are you the one they assigned to help me."

"Help you?"

"With the baby."

"Nope. I have first dibs on Charlotte."

"First dibs?"

"It took me three hours, but I won the Heads or Tail competition. That means I get to spend the first hour with Charlotte." Fred removes a burp cloth from one pocket and slaps it onto his shoulder, removes a tiny, lamb-shaped baby rattle from the other pocket and gives it a shake, "I'm all set, so hand her over."

"Thank God."

"What was that?" Fred chuckles.

"Nothing." Manuel walks to Fred and places the baby carrier onto the ground. Then he amazes at the ease with which Fred unbuckles Charlotte from the carrier, lifts her – whilst doing the whole support the head and neck thing – and cradles her in his arms with a tiny kiss to her cheek. Then Daddy listens in as Fred coos to the tiny bundle.

"First things first; always choose heads – heads – tails, in a Heads or Tail coin toss. Second, I've got stories about your daddy, so here's the deal, Miss Charlotte, when you mess up, or step over the line, or break curfew, come find me. I'm sure I've got something about that nervous dude over there that will even the score. And another thing. Don't let anyone at The Compound scold you for lying. Everyone here lies — almost as often as they breathe." Fred laughs big. Places a kiss to Charlotte's head and gives his seal of approval, "She's perfect, Manuel."

The dumbfounded daddy watches as Fred walks away with the newborn. "You've got one hour, Mr. Mom," Manuel calls after the doting detective, then turns to the only one still standing outside, "Are you ready to deal with your shit, Malcolm?"

"I am."

The killer sends these?

The men head to a guest cottage set several hundred feet into heavy woods. Manuel shuts the door behind them and starts in. "Gretchen still doesn't know about Sage Finley?"

"No, but she's been checking me out on the internet."

"She told you?"

"No. She commented on a picture in my game room and recognized it as being the shot taken right before I blew out my knee. She had to have seen it online."

"If she's doing research, it's just a matter of time before she reads something about your rumored association with the call girl. I went online and searched your name so I have a sense about what Gretchen has been looking at. The first few hundred articles were about your game, particularly your last game, but there's stuff there about Sage – and you – and Wyldwood. Gretchen's gonna be all up in that shit as soon as she learns there was another woman and that she was murdered on your property. I also spent time searching Sage Finley – once Gretchen comes across Sage's name and focuses her searches on her, there's enough to keep her busy, there are plenty of rumors about the two of you."

"Rumors don't bother me, Manuel, these do." Malcolm reaches into his travel bag and removes an envelope. He hands it to the former Fed, "There are nearly a dozen other envelopes just like that at my place."

Manuel removes a set of pictures – they tell the horrific story of Sage Finley's last moments on earth...

Sage Finley was sprawled on the floor; her body half in, half out of her garden cottage in an ever-spreading pool of blood. Her eyes were locked onto clay pots full of beautiful flowers. Colorful little innocents that sat in stark contrast to the shiny wet crimson splatter that ran the length of walls and soaked into the cushions of overturned furniture that she banged against in her attempt to flee – to live.

The slumbering young woman unlocked and opened her door without asking who was on the other side. "I'm coming," she said when a knock pulled her from the couch, "I fell asleep and was having the most wonderful dream..." Sage had been warned about the door...

"Keep the door locked, the security on, and don't open the door to anyone but me ... don't open the door to anyone ... don't open ..."

The beautiful young woman with the wide toothy smile and happy future ahead heeded those warnings before – but she had fallen asleep – and she forgot – and she was expecting her man at the door – the man who rescued her – and loved her — not the one who burst in and began savagely raging her. Tiny flashes of light and odd clicking sounds filled the last bits of her consciousness. As she struggled to stay on this side of life, Sage Finley watched Micky Strong casually walk out her terrace doors. A warm August breeze moved through those doors – it found her and lovingly caressed her.

Malcolm…is that you…Momma

Sage Finley's last words may have passed her lips or drifted as a thought. They most definitely moved in concert with her eyes as they fixed and dilated upon the clay pots full of beautiful flowers she lovingly tended to that afternoon.

Manuel grimaces. "Fuck man. The killer sends these?"

"The killer is Micky Strong, and yes, he sends a set every year. They're postmarked August 1st and arrive on or near the anniversary of Sage's murder."

Manuel finishes flipping through the grotesque images, puts them back into the envelope, and tucks it into his back pocket. "When I came to Wyldwood in 2017 to talk to you about the hacker-for-hire case against Stoner Strong, you'd already received multiple sets of these pictures?"

"Yes and no. Multiple sets had been sent to me, but I didn't know about them until I got back to Lewisburg. After Sage died, I checked out mentally. I did two things: I played basketball and I worked the ranch. Jason handled my business stuff, but anything that looked like it was personal in nature, condolence cards, anything hand-addressed, that kind of stuff was put aside and stored at my condo at Alamo Heights. That's why I didn't see the first few envelopes. The rest were sent to Wyldwood. Sammi set my mail aside during my…"

"…Time away," Manuel finishes Malcolm's sentence for him.

"I was going to say, during my disintegration."

Manuel nods – pauses. "So Sammi gave these to you when you got back from Vancouver?"

"She handed me a duffle bag full of correspondence when I left Texas."

"Why didn't you deal with this back then – when you first got back to Lewisburg?"

Malcolm knows there isn't a good answer, so he goes with the truth. "I barely made it through losing Sage and the game. After I dealt with that mind-fuck, I knew I needed to stay in the present so I could stay whole. I really believed I'd only be successful if I didn't talk about Sage. I never said a word about her, about us. I wouldn't be talking about her now, but…"

"Something's happened. What happened?" Manuel pushes.

"Gretchen…"

"What?" Gretchen says from the cottage doorway putting an abrupt end to the conversation.

"Wasn't talking to you Woman, just about you," Malcolm playfully growls.

"Well, then, let me rephrase my question." She waits a beat. "Why?"

"Come here, Woman." He wraps his arms around her. "See yourself out, Manuel."

Seal the deal.

Just having his woman near, settles him, seizes him. Malcolm's need presses hard against her. She gently pushes him away. The rarely rebuffed man runs his hand down her arm and takes hold of her hand. She pulls away. "Everything okay, Woman?"

Gretchen gets all lawyerly, "Let's get settled, then you and I need to talk."

The two silently cross-current one another through unfamiliar space; one trying to avoid the sage colored elephant in the room, the other trying to plan their upcoming conversation.

Malcolm puts some physical distance by heading to the kitchen for bottled water. "Want one?"

"I'm good thanks." Gretchen gears up for a word mash as she makes her way to the fireplace across the living room, "I love the open floor plan, and the whiteness of it all. Sheer brilliance on the decorator's part having most everything be in white. It could be dark and gloomy in here otherwise, especially since the floors are graphite tile – the white brightens without blinding." She moves to the master suite and calls out, "This place is beautiful, Malcolm, a complete reversal of the living room color scheme."

When he arrives the room is empty. "Woman?"

"In the en suite," she calls out again.

He moves to the doorway and watches her flit about. He steps into the room, "Excuse me," he says as he leans into the shower and turns it on. He steps to Gretchen and starts undressing her. She starts returning the favor, then abruptly stops.

"We need to talk."

"You're killing me, Woman."

Gretchen puts a little space between them. "I need a minute; I'll meet you in the bedroom." She shuts off the shower with shaking hand, stands in front of the mirror, and readies herself mentally. "Present the facts, then work it through. There's a solution to every problem," she whispers. "I really hope he doesn't think this is a problem."

Malcolm is leaning against the far wall by the bed when Gretchen enters the room. His feet are crossed at the ankles, his fingers are tapping his cell phone, he stops when he sees the expression on his woman's face. "Gretchen," he pushes from the wall to join her.

She raises her hand. "Don't move."

"Woman, talk to me."

She pulls a deep cleansing breath and walks to him. She hands him a plastic circular dispenser and walks away.

"Are these…?"

"Birth control pills."

"Tell me more."

"Those are for the month of May. As you can see, I only took a couple, and the last one I took was on the day Cappa Escobar tried to kill me in the garage. Add that nightmare to Manuel's custody battle, and the shooting of Escobar at your place, and it adds up to a whopping, 'I forgot to take my birth control pills'. I realized it when we packed for the trip," she finishes on a shaky breath and budding tears.

"Woman, can I move, now?"

Gretchen nods.

He walks to her and places his gigantic hand onto her abdomen. "Are you pregnant?"

"I don't know," she sobs.

"And if you are?"

Gretchen lifts her cornflower blue eyes to her man's hoping she finds acceptance of the situation—she does. The corner of her lips turn ever so slightly upward.

Malcolm pulls her to him. "Woman, if it's all the same to you I'd like to press into you for a while and seal the deal."

Gretchen's smile widens as big, wet happy tears roll.

He leads her to the shower and gentles her until she's breathless and begging. He pats her dry still working her breathless parts then takes her to bed. "Don't talk," he whispers. Malcolm straddles Gretchen's legs. He keeps his weight off her belly as he kisses, sucks, and strokes. He feels each lift of her hips as she silently calls him home. He kisses, sucks, and strokes her to within a whisper of orgasm.

"Malcolm, please," she pants.

He inches in, then presses the rest of the way, leaving every bit of himself inside when her satisfaction tightens around him. He rolls off and pulls Gretchen into his spoon. She begins to weep. He pulls her tighter against him. "Woman, talk to me."

"I love you."

"I know that, Gretchen."

"It was fun love before," she sobs.

"And now?"

"It's so deep it hurts." Gretchen pulls a few shaky breaths before speaking again. "Malcolm, I hope you sealed the deal."

Malcolm rolls her beneath him. "Woman, you've completely undone me."

You didn't sign up for this.

Manuel enters his cottage and finds his **very** new romantic fling, Muriel Dermot, rocking his sleeping baby. He takes a long look at the woman and wonders if there is a future for them – he knows there isn't. "As pretty a picture as this is, Muriel, we need to talk."

She nods. "Follow me," she whispers.

The cottage Manuel shares with Muriel is identical to the guest cottage Gretchen and Malcolm are in. When Manuel follows Muriel to the master bedroom, he expects to find a walk-in closet where a walk-in closet is supposed to be. Muriel delights in his surprise. "Steve and Mike converted most of the closet space into a nursery. It will have to make do until an addition can be added to the place," Muriel whisper-explains.

Manuel enters his daughter's nursery. He stands in awe of the space and the tiny furnishings. After a minute or two, he moves about, running his fingertips over silk and satin trimmed baby things—pink and white baby things.

"We painted the walls, sage," Muriel whispers proudly, "I think it's a lovely contrast color."

Sage. There's that word again, he silently acknowledges.

Manuel watches, admiringly, as Muriel puts Charlotte into an eyelet lace trimmed stroller-type bassinet, and places a finger-kiss to her forehead. She grabs one of two baby monitors from the changing table and leads Manuel out of the room.

"What the hell was that?" Manuel mimics the whole whisper-talking thing. "You know how to do kids?"

"Do kids? Whatever does that mean, Manuel?" Muriel laughs full-on when they get back to the living room.

"Don't go parsing my words, Muriel, you just did that baby girl right with all the rocking, and holding, and finger-touch kissing, and baby monitor remembering. Is there some sort of manual that explains all that?"

"I suppose there are manuals, but I used to babysit the Phillips kids when I was in high school. I guess I picked up a few things."

Manuel pulls Muriel into his arms. "You didn't sign up for this."

"Neither did you," she nudges, "I suppose it's discussion and decision time, then." Muriel kisses his cheek and moves to the couch.

He doesn't join her. He moves across the room and leans against a little sitting ledge at the front windows. "I need a minute to think, Muriel." His thoughts take him back to the first time he laid eyes on her…

The missing and once-presumed dead writer was holed up in her sculpting studio when the men arrived at Pickering Farm. *Sympathy for the Devil* was blaring from inside. Even with Jagger's deafening decibels, Muriel's off-key singalong reverberated. The detectives, accompanied by an artist, and an uncle, watched as the young woman twirled throughout the room. As she passed by the sculpting table she pounded her fits against a massive mound of clay. In that moment, the artist known as Christine Marsden was a free-dancing, free-sculpting gypsy who was using every inch of her room and every ounce of herself in the creative process. The whirling dervish screeched to a halt when she caught movement from the corner of her eye.

"Frank – Jackson," the words caught on an exhale. Her expression changed from delight to dread at the sight of the two strange men standing there. Her last bit of motion ended with her layered hair coming to rest in a mess of waves around her face and chest. She ran her fingers through it and quickly twirled it atop her head. Her round cobalt blue eyes moistened, her lips pinched then widened into her best reassuring smile. She forgot all else and connected with the men she loves, dearly. "Looks like the jig is up," she said as she walked toward the group. The woman threw her arms around her crestfallen uncle and whispered, "Don't worry Uncle Frank, it's for the best." She stepped away from his embrace and extended her hand to the strangers, "Until two minutes ago, I was Christine Marsden, a recluse living on an island in Penobscot Bay. Since you men look like you might be of the hunting breed, you probably know that I am Muriel Dermot."

Fred Serpico identified himself and shook her hand, "Ms. Dermot, it's a pleasure to meet you."

A hunk named Manuel Xavier took her hand, "Ms. Dermot, you might want to cover your…" he motioned his fingers in the general direction of her boobs.

She glanced downward. Her sweaty white tank top was clinging to her braless form and her nipples WERE. ON. BLAST. She quickly untied the chambray shirt from around her waist and slipped it on. "Thank you, Mr. Xavier. Most guys would have enjoyed the show."

"I'm one of those guys, Ms. Dermot, but I'm also a gentleman."

Muriel needed Manuel then—he needs her now. "Muriel, we met in April, I found out about Charlotte in May, it's June and she's sleeping in a closet in my bedroom. It's a lot for me, it has to be freaking you out."

Muriel shrugs, "It is what it is, Manuel." She gets up and moves to him – he spreads his legs – she leans in. "I spent the better part of the last two years being hunted by a serial killer; an itty-bitty baby doesn't scare me. You and I have feelings for one another, maybe those feelings will grow, maybe they won't. Charlotte being part of our equation certainly raises the stakes. Let me bottom-line this; you are that sweet baby's father, and you need to bond with her. I'm here to help out for as long as we want to be together."

Manuel isn't sure at that particular moment if he wants her or needs her, but he takes her.

What's HE like in bed?

A welcoming breakfast is held at the Main Cottage at 10 AM. The place is packed to the rafters – it's not every day a basketball legend visits The Compound. The host of that morning's gathering, Rocco Fiancetti, welcomes everyone. The founder of RFI is a suave, crushingly good-looking scoundrel. The former British Intelligence officer commands the room, and easily annoys his team with his kitschy Italian vocabulary and ridiculous "knick-knack-name introductions."

"Ms. Mitchell, Mr. Price, I, Rocco Fiancetti bid welcomes and introductions." He points in succession, first to Joy Fiancetti, "my Only One," to Fred Serpico, "the Detecting One," to Kitt Mahoney, "the Writing One," to Steve Phelps, "the Rambling One," to Maura Putnam, "the Flowering One and with her is the Budding One," to Annie Mahoney-Maxwell, "the Piccolo One," to Michael Monopoli, "the Woodsy One," to John Maxwell, "the Annoying One," to Hannah Leavy, "the Decadent One," to Manuel Xavier, "the Offspringing One," to Muriel Dermot, "the Murdering One," and to Tess and Callie, "the Twinning Ones."

As each of the assembled is introduced, there is wave of a hand and a roll of the eyes for their host. Malcolm and Gretchen find it all very amusing until they're assigned "knick-knack-names" of their own.

"Ms. Mitchell you will be the Bleaching One and Mr. Price you will be the Dribbling One."

Malcolm suppresses his growl. Sort of. "If anyone other than our host calls me the Dribbling One, I am going to be the very Pissed-Off One," he warns. There is a collective nod of the head, and a big laugh from Every One!

The welcomed guests formally introduce themselves to Rocco and Joy Fiancetti then head to Fred Serpico. "Detecting One, it is good to see you again," Malcolm says with a broad smile and outstretched hand. Fred introduces his fiancée, "Kitt Mahoney, this is Gretchen Mitchell and..."

"77. It's a pleasure to meet you both."

Malcolm nudges Gretchen who rolls her eyes at her man, "Yeah, yeah, everyone knows 77." She touches Kitt's arm, "Are you the writer of *Bullet Bungalow?*" Kitt nods and smiles. Gretchen smiles wide. "I've heard great things about your novel. I can't wait to give it a read."

Malcolm does a bit of grousing, "The woman knows the writer," he turns away with a shake of the head, and is rewarded with the whispered snickering of 15-year-old faux twins. He nods in their direction. "I hear the Twinning Ones have game."

The tittering stops and the girls get serious. "Enough," Tess says with confidence.

Malcolm smiles wide. "Bring it."

In unison they say, "Consider it brung," then go back to their whispering and snickering.

The Bleaching One and the Dribbling One circle the room then partake in an incredible breakfast prepared by the Piccolo One. After breakfast, the gender sets split—the men go on a tour of the Compound—the women talk about the men who go on a tour of the Compound.

A very expectant, Maura Putnam, calls out to Gretchen from a comfy couch that appears to have swallowed her whole. "Did you really not know who 77 was when you met him?"

Gretchen laughs and nods.

"Damn, that must have been one hell of a rock you were under," Maura's laugh quickly turns to a moan, "These darn babies just won't get off my bladder..." She stops cold when she realizes what she's said.

"Babies!" Kitt, Joy, Annie, Leavy, Callie and Tess scream in unison.

Gretchen tenses from the sudden outburst.

"Oh, shit," Maura snaps. "I almost made it to delivery keeping the secret. I wanted to surprise you all."

Kitt walks to the back of the couch and wraps her arms around her best friend since preschool. "Consider me surprised and thrilled. Do you know what the babies are?"

"Yes, but it's going to be a surprise even if I have to tape my mouth shut!"

Callie and Tess decide they'd rather spend time at the hoops than talking about babies. No sooner has the screen door slammed behind them when the women get down and dirty with Gretchen. Actually, it's Maura who gets down and dirty, "What's HE like in bed?"

Every woman turns disbelieving eyes to the feisty redhead. "What? I'm allowed," Maura defends.

Kitt snickers. "Because you're pregnant?"

"Because I'm nosey. Spill it oh, Bleaching One," Maura laughs.

"Gentle," Gretchen says on a swoon.

The women return her swoon, and go all in with an "Ahhhhh."

"What about marriage and kids?" Maura pushes.

Gretchen shifts uncomfortably in her seat—fights the tears that suddenly spring.

There is silence. Maura breaks the silence. "Gretchen are you pregnant?" the newly licensed physician's assistant asks tenderly.

The Decadent One leans toward the Writing One and says, "Maura's 'knick-knack' name should be changed to the Intrusive One."

The Bleaching One who is now the Crying One shakes her head. "I don't know." Five minutes later, she's explained the birth control pill fiasco.

Kitt Mahoney scoffs, "Been there, done that. His name is Joseph."

Everyone laughs, except Maura, she hoists herself from her seat and takes control. "If you're pregnant, you need prenatal care. Come on, let's go find out."

The women follow a waddling Maura to the Medical Center. Once inside, the women wait while Gretchen pees on a stick – for the stick to do its thing – and for Gretchen's response – to the results that appear on the stick – that did its thing.

Hoops and hackers?

The entire Compound gathers around the basketball court for fun and games that afternoon. Malcolm makes note that the tittering 15-year-old girls he met that morning are gone. In their place are two serious b-ballers. The opponents meet at center court, shake hands and commence with a three-person game of H-O-R-S-E. Malcolm, Callie, and Tess make every one of their shots from different locations around the key ending the game with no declared winner. The threesome picks up the pace with a fierce 2 on 1 game where the girls work their stealing and passing skills. Malcolm pulls back on his "everything" until the girls are up 10 to 4 in an 11-point game, then he puts IT on the floor bringing the game to a 10-10 tie that the girls break for the win. The crowd erupts. Callie and Tess tap Malcolm on his shoulder and end their fun and games with an in unison, "Maybe next time, 77."

Malcolm laughs big.

The game-day ends with drills that include lots of coaching by Malcolm and lots of learning by the girls. Two hours later Malcolm is talking with the Mahoney-Maxwell-Serpico clan about the girls' game. "Callie and Tess have the skills and the temperament. They can easily pull college scholarships. I'm impressed," he says before heading for a shower. As he walks away, he hears the girls' tittering. It's full-on.

Before reaching the heavy tree line, Malcolm sees Gretchen standing at the edge of Roseway river, a beautiful waterway that runs along the edge of The Compound. He starts toward her, stops when Manuel pulls him up short. "There's an office on the lower level of the headquarters. Shower then find it." A half-hour later Malcolm walks in and finds Rocco and Manuel deep in conversation.

"Ah, the Dribbling One has arrived."

Manuel drops his head and groans.

Malcolm growls.

Rocco ignores and extends his hand toward a seat. "Sit, si?"

"I'll stand." Malcolm finds a wall and does his thing.

Manuel jumps in. "I called my former boss, Director Stacy Remington at FICA and asked for the investigative file on the hacker-for-hire, Stoner Strong. The Director had the field office in San Antonio send it and a few other things over. She hasn't asked why I want it, but she will. Once she puts the pieces together and figures out this case is about you, she's going to connect you to Gretchen and Gretchen to Granger, and since Stacy Remington and Granger Mitchell are tight, there's gonna be talk between the two. Eventually, a related talk will take place between the father and daughter. The shit is gonna hit the fan, sooner or later, so it's best we find out as much as we can, as fast as we can."

Malcolm nods.

Manuel starts with some background, mostly for Rocco's benefit. "Stoner Strong was my first FICA investigation…"

FICA Quadrant Manager, Kristen Millie, handed several files to Agent Manuel Xavier. He read the name at the top of the first file, "Wendell 'Stoner' Strong."

"Mr. Strong is a hacker-for-hire in Texas. He lives in San Antonio, but works statewide. He's been on our radar since 2007, when he did a deep dive on Malcolm Price. FICA Director Gaffney ordered that there be no victim notification made while Price and the Spurs were in the hunt for the NBA Title. That decision has caused me some sleepless nights."

"How so?"

"Stoner Strong's uncle is Micky Strong…"

"Ma'am?"

"Micky Strong was a PI in the San Antonio area. More to the point, he is being sought for the murder of Sage Finley, the former girlfriend of Malcolm Price. Familiarize yourself with the files, Agent Xavier, then pack your bags. You're going to San Antonio for the duration. Do not come back to DC until Wendell 'Stoner' Strong is behind bars. I'll toss in a month's vacation if you can get Micky Strong."

"On it, ma'am."

"I put together a solid case proving Stoner was a hacker-for-hire. The Feds were more interested in the people up the food chain so we offered Stoner reduced charges if he'd flip on them. The only part of our case where he held his tongue was the Malcolm Price hacking. He said **nothing**. We let him know we had proof he dove into Malcolm's shit twice in 2007. The first dive netted him financials, professional contracts, emails, and phone numbers. The second dive was more of a surface swim. flight schedules, entertainment bookings, that sort of thing."

Malcolm drops his head, "Micky paid Stoner to find out when Sage would be alone."

Manuel grunts. "Yeah." He moves to the wall opposite Malcolm and directs some attitude his way. "After Stoner's hacking arrest, I went to Wyldwood and pushed you for answers. You gave me nothing." Manuel gives Malcolm a minute then lays the truth bare. "The original murder investigation stalled in 2007 because no one 'knew' Malcolm Price had a thing with Sage Finley. There were rumors, lots of rumors, but no one would go on the record. People from San Antonio to Wyldwood, and everywhere in between, buttoned up for you, Malcolm."

He nods.

Manuel holds up two stapled pieces of paper. The heading, **San Antonio Police**

Department is easily readable from where Malcolm stands. "This is the report filed by Detective Romney. He interviewed you a few weeks after Sage Finley's murder. I'm gonna read it to you."

"You don't need to read it, Manuel, I remember every fucking word. Read the questions. I'll give you the same answers today that I gave that night."

Manuel shoots a dubious look his papa's way. Rocco shrugs, "Let's see how he does." Manuel reads the questions.

"Did you know Sage Finley?"

"I did."

"Was she a paid escort?"

"She was."

"Was she a paid escort of yours?"

"No, she was not."

"When did you learn she was in that line of work?"

"At the beginning of the playoffs. Micky Strong, a private investigator in San Antonio, brought her to a Spurs meet and greet. She was his escort that night."

"And she ended up living near your ranch in Wyldwood. Care to explain?"

"No."

Manuel reads the rest of the transcript, they are detective Romney's words. "Fine. Let me tell you what we know. **We know** that Micky

Strong introduced you to his 'working girl' at a meet and greet. **We know** that your right-hand-man, Jason Carpenter invited them to the meet and greet at your request. **We know** that Micky mouthed off that you took Sage Finley from him that night. **We know** that you and the former hooker were the singular focus of the PI for months. **We know** that Micky Strong paid a hacker to get information on you. **We know** that he found your secret ranch. **We know** that he was seen up in Wyldwood prior to the murder of Ms. Finley. **We know** he left his life behind in July and hasn't been seen or heard from since August 5. **We know** that Sage Finley was hacked to pieces in a sweet little cottage paid for by you. And **we know** that there is a lot more to this story."

Manuel tosses the papers onto the desk. "Nice recall on the dialogue. Now let's recap. In 2007, a murdered escort you stole from her regular customer ended up dead in a cottage a stone's throw from your ranch. You didn't help with the initial murder investigation; some might even say you obstructed it. In 2017, FICA was all-up in the shit of Stoner Strong. He was facing jail time for a bunch of nuisance hacks, but we wanted him for the work he did for his PI uncle – the same uncle whose former hooker was hacked to death in a cottage a stone's throw from your ranch See the full circle here?"

Manuel stares.

Malcolm nods.

Manuel continues. "If you hadn't pissed on my investigation back in 2017, I could have squeezed the fuck out of Stoner Strong. I could have threatened accessory before the fact in a first-degree murder case. I could have forced his hand and made him flip on Micky Strong. **If** you had helped with my investigation." Manuel gets a rise from Malcolm.

"Old news, Manuel! My secrets are coming home to roost very soon. I'll deal with the fallout—I deserve to deal with the fallout. But Micky Strong needs to be found and he needs to pay for what he did to Sage!"

"Agreed," Manuel takes a breath then breaks into a smile. "Some things have changed. There's some leverage now."

Malcolm pushes off the wall and takes a seat, "Talk to me, Manuel."

"Stoner is currently serving a ten-year sentence at a place in Waco. A year or so after he went in, the San Antonio FBI field office received a call from Stoner's girlfriend – his very pissed-off girlfriend. Chelsea Brady accused Stoner of being a cheating bastard and told the Feds she has something they may be interested in having. That something was a key to a San Antonio storage unit originally rented by Micky Strong. The unit is still held in Micky's name, but it was being paid for by Stoner. When he ended up behind bars, Chelsea started making the payments."

Malcom gets up and goes back to his wall.

Manuel continues. "Given that Micky is the prime suspect in the homicide of Sage Finley, the Feds go in and look around the unit. There isn't much of Micky's stuff there, certainly nothing that will help prove he killed Sage, but there is plenty of stuff to tie Micky to Stoner and Stoner to you." Manuel lets Malcolm process while he takes a sip of soda. He can feel Malcolm begin to seethe while he waits.

"Manuel," he growls.

The Fiancetti men shoot smiles at Malcolm. "Stoner left a record of all the hacking work he did over the years to help Micky with his PI business. The record details payments Stoner received for his work on you. He received a thousand bucks for the deep dive on you in the spring of 2007, and another five-grand for the reconnaissance dive on you in the summer of 2007."

Malcolm shakes his head in disgust. "Micky upped Stoner's pay after the dick made bank betting on the Spurs in the 2007 Finals."

Manuel nods. "There's more. Stoner has been getting five-grand every July beginning in 2008."

"Payments for sending me the pictures of Sage," Malcolm exhales.

Manuel nods, and then drops the prize, "Stoner is behind bars. That means someone else sent one of the sets to you."

"Now what?" Malcolm asks.

"We start investigating, Hard. When we get a lead on Micky, we go in and put a noose around Stoner's neck. We make him see that giving Micky up is his only option."

Malcolm heads for the door. "You need to do this fast, Manuel."

"Why?"

"I'm declaring my candidacy for Mayor of Lewisburg on August 1st."

Manuel and Rocco shoot looks. Manuel states the obvious, "Timing sucks, Malcolm."

Rocco Fiancetti speaks for the first time. "You need to tell Ms. Mitchell of this situation. Be warned of this, Mr. Price, she won't see past your silence if she learns of this from another. She is a fierce woman, why do you choose not to tell her?"

"Gretchen might be pregnant. Find Micky," Malcolm says on his way out of the office.

Easy-go-fucky.

Mick Stone formerly known as Micky Strong adds an orange slice and lime rind to the fifteenth Belladonna, he's made that day. Mick Stone is owner and operator of Mick's on the Beach, a wildly popular tiki-bar on Playa Los Cerritos, a wildly popular beach on the Province of Los Santos in Panama. On the day the new and marginally-improved version of Micky Strong arrived in Central America, the little tiki-bar went up for sale. His tagalong broad went on and on that it was 'divine intervention' but Mick wasn't a believer, and more to the point, he was a murderer who needed to hide, and needed something to do to fill his time, so he figured he'd buy the place. It was the perfect setup since the only things Micky/Mick knew was being a private dick, being an all-around dick, playing the books, playing with whores, and drinking in bars. He also figured buying a tiki-bar with money he made betting on 77 and the Spurs was a perfect ending to his days in San Antonio – and his naming it, Mick's on the Beach, well, that was a perfect tip of the hat to his favorite haunt back home, Paula's on the Chase.

The bartender puts the fruity mixed drink in front of a regular customer and looks out at the sand and surf. He easily spots his beachcombing whore amongst the bevy of babes. He waits for her to feel his stare, then sends her a wave. The one thing about leaving San Antonio that makes life almost enjoyable is Cloe Fishbaum, the buxom blonde who came along for his ride. The original Micky Strong picked Cloe up from Garden of Eve, a San Antonio escort service, the night of a 2007 Spurs playoff game and never brought her back. He's had a good long run with the easy-go-fucky Cloe. "Give her a couple drinks, a day on the beach, a few gossip magazines, and the internet, and she's the happiest whore alive," he says with a salute of the whiskey part of a boilermaker. Mick knows his good long run with Cloe will end one day. "I'm playing a long game with Malcolm Price, and when the game goes into overtime, there's gonna be hell to pay. Nobody will come out unscathed," he says while working a beer chaser.

I need a favor.

Fred Serpico spends long hours inside the Athletic Center of late. He's still doing a little rehab work after getting injured during the Who-What-When-Where-Why serial killer case. A bullet to the shoulder and an antique sofa to the back put Fred in the Medical Center for treatment and in the Athletic Center for physical therapy. That's where he's been since the b-ball tourney between the star athlete and doppelganger teens ended. While there, Fred has watched Malcolm Price head to the guest cottage, presumably to shower after the skirmish, head to the lower level office, presumably for a meeting, and then back to the basketball court, where he's been pounding the shit out of the boards – and himself. "Doesn't take a detective to figure out something's up," the detective mumbles as he does his umpteenth lap. After a shower, Fred heads outside. He takes a seat on the bleachers and watches the legendary 77 leave it all on the floor. "Yeah, something's up."

From Shelburne to Halifax
Manuel and Leavy are headed out on a mail run. Normally, Mike Monopoli handles the hour+ trip to a hangar at the Halifax airport to get deliveries. Given that The Compound is a secure location, communications are usually handled electronically, but select mailings travel

a mapped route through a mail center in DC, then are flown to the peninsula. The reason Mike is not on this mail run is because he is up to his ass in survivalist training with U.K. recruits. Forty trainees are currently dispersed across the 105-acre property, with nothing more than minimal provisions, and a temporary tattoo that's a replica of a series of hashmarks on trees, that if followed correctly will lead the recruits to—and not away from the Main Cottage. So, while Mike is monitoring and rescuing, Manuel and Leavy are driving and gathering.

"What's the rush with this mail run?" Manuel asks, as his ass meets leather seat.

"There's a special delivery for Malcolm Price, a letter and a courier package."

"Huh."

"Huh, what?" Leavy pushes. Leavy gets no response. Leavy turns off the radio.

"Hey, I was listening to that."

"The Red Hot Chili Peppers can wait. I, on the other hand cannot. Spill it, Manuel."

"Spill what?" Manual laughs. Manuel gets no response. Manuel spills it. "Price has a situation. First, a little background. My first investigation at FICA was a hacker-for-hire investigation in San Antonio."

The Compound
Malcolm enters the guest cottage after a protracted time on the court, a long talk with

Fred, and another shower at the Athletic Center. He smiles w.i.d.e. when he hears his woman screeching her anthem from the shower. He laughs because He knows that She knows he owns her. "You own me too, Gretchen," he admits. Malcolm tosses a set of keys onto the kitchen counter. They land next to two pieces of mail addressed to him. One is an envelope from the City of Lewisburg, Pennsylvania, the other is an unmarked package. He knows what it is and who sent it. When the water stops running, he heads to the bedroom carrying the deliveries. The waiting man has been swallowed by one of two marshmallow chairs in the sitting area, when Gretchen walks out of the bathroom. He notices her hand; it's placed lightly on her belly covering a tiny baby bump beneath. He knows she is pregnant; he knew it last night when he was in her. He wants to take her in his arms and tell her how happy he is, but he doesn't want to rob her of telling him the news, so he waits.

"Malcolm, you're back," she startles a bit then smiles wide showing her joy.

"Never left, Woman."

"I'm thinking we should stay in tonight, just hang out, if that's all right?" She smiles even wider.

Malcolm nods.

"Good. I'm cooking our omelet," she tosses her best sexy smile over her shoulder and leaves the room.

Malcolm thinks back to the first time Gretchen cooked an omelet for him. It was after their first sexual encounter when Gretchen came seeking Malcolm's help with a favor and they ended up in his bed…

Malcolm bent his 6'5" frame and leaned his arm on the roof of her car. "Get lost going home the other day, Counselor?" He said through a million-watt smile.

Gretchen matched his million-watt smile with one of her own, "I need a favor."

"I hope that's code for your wanting me to bang your brains out," Malcolm playfully growls.

Gretchen tossed her platinum hair, and with a laugh, "I have every intention of banging your brains out, but I do need a favor."

Malcolm stood tall and pointed to a space next to his Mercedes. "Park your Diamond White next to my Magnetite Black, but don't get out of your car unless you're sure about us." Malcolm was leaning against his car when She. Stepped. Out. He was taken aback by her appearance. Gone was the lawyer's pencil-skirt-blazer-combo that he'd become accustomed. This vixen was wearing a peak-a-boo white gauze peasant shirt, pair of bootcut, hip hugging jeans, and pair of scuffed ankle high, stiletto heel cowboy boots. A smile creased his face. "Well, look at you. Just when I thought I had you all figured out, you go and shake it all up. Damn you're one fine piece of work, Gretchen."

~

Gretchen scrambled eggs with feta cheese and spinach, Malcolm opened a bottle of Señor Sangria Classic White. They sat across from each other, she dressed in one of his long-sleeved T-shirts that hit her mid-thigh, he in a pair of sweats that hung l.o.w. on his hips.

"Why do you work at the prison?" she asked.

"Penitentiary," he corrected.

"Seriously, Malcolm, I'd like to know why."

"Are you asking me why I work at all or why I work there in particular?"

"There."

"I'm at the women's wing of the penitentiary because there are too many men behind bars who would love to make a name by killing a former NBA star."

Gretchen nodded. "Now for the other question, why are you working a nine to five job at all?"

"I have plans for later in life, so while I wait for later, I'm earning an honest day's pay for an honest day's work."

"Do you feel like sharing what your 'later in life' plans are?"

"Politics," was all he said.

"Really?" Gretchen said a bit too quickly and holding the *eeeee* a tad too long.

"You seem surprised, Gretchen."

"Well, yeah, you're way too nice for politics, although you're banging hot, so you'll get the women's vote."

Malcolm smiled. "What makes you think I'm way too nice, Counselor?"

"You loved me gently," Gretchen whispered.

Malcolm got up from the table and took Gretchen's hand. "Come on, Woman, I want to gentle you some more."

Gretchen's call from the kitchen pulls Malcolm from his memories. He takes the envelopes and answers her call.

"Oh, I was wondering where those envelopes went. The Decadent One said the small one was delivered by courier and the other one came registered mail." Gretchen walks two omelet-filled plates to the kitchen table. "Let's eat, I'm starved."

"You eat, Woman, I'll talk." Malcolm waits until she's halfway through her omelet before opening the envelope that came registered mail. He takes out several documents and hands them to Gretchen. She reads the top line of the first page and turns wide cornflower blue eyes to him. "Intent to file for Candidacy, for Mayor of Lewisburg? Your little borough has a mayor; his term doesn't end until 2022."

"Mayor Jack Cane is retiring due to illness. It will be announced July 1st. A special election will be scheduled for the first Tuesday in

November. I've been asked to run and I need to file those papers by August 1st if I'm throwing my hat in."

Gretchen hands the papers back. "Of course you're running. This is your dream."

"Governor is my dream."

"You said I'm your dream," Gretchen teases as she crawls onto her man's lap.

"Every night, Woman." He presses against her bottom. "Let's eat later." Malcolm takes Gretchen to bed and gentles her until the stars come out. Just before midnight Malcolm whispers into Gretchen's ear, "You awake, Woman?"

"I am now," she giggles.

He wraps her tight and places his hand on top of hers which is resting gently on her baby bump. "You've undone me, Gretchen. Do you think you might want to undo me forever?"

Gretchen turns toward him. "Longer than forever."

Malcolm reaches under his pillow and removes a black box. He holds it hidden in his hand. "Can you put the light on?"

Gretchen laughs, "I can, but do I want to?"

"I want to check my knee. I think I twisted it shooting hoops."

Malcolm is sitting when she turns back. "Woman, I need a favor."

She smiles wide, "I hope that's code for your wanting me to bang your brains out,"

"Always," he laughs, "but I want a bit more than that." He takes hold of her hand, "Gretchen, I want you more than I need you, and I need you more than anything in this world. I hope you'll be my wife." Malcolm opens the black box he's been holding, and presents Gretchen with a seven-carat, radiant cut, cornflower blue sapphire, platinum banded ring. Gretchen's matching cornflower blue eyes fill with tears as he slips the ring onto her finger.

"Yes, I'll be Mrs. 77. That is your number, right?"

Malcolm laughs big. He relaxes back and watches his woman as she admires the ring.

"It's the most beautiful thing I've ever seen. You know, Malcolm, cornflower blue sapphires are very rare. Princess Diana had one, but hers had deep violet undertones, this one is blue through and through. Where on earth did you find it?"

"Sotheby's."

"In Geneva?" she croaks. "Oh. My. God. Is this one of *the* Burmese sapphires?"

"Woman, just enjoy it."

"Oh. My. God. It's a Burmese sapphire. Oh. My. God. This is one of the most rarified stones in the world. Do you know what this is worth? Of course you know what it's worth you just bought it. Malcolm, we need to get this insured. Maybe I shouldn't wear it..."

Malcolm pulls his Woman beneath him, she scrambles away. "Wait, here. I have something blue for you, too." Gretchen runs naked to the front room and then back. She snuggles in bed next to Malcolm and hands him the pregnancy test showing a blue equal sign.

The beaming man places one of his hands onto Gretchen's baby bump and the other onto his heart. "Woman, you've undone me forever."

Empty spoons and fractured hearts.

The RFI Learjet landed at Fox Hollow Airport just before noon on July 1st. After weeks away, Malcolm, Gretchen and their guest, Manuel Xavier, arrive at 275 Market Street in time to watch Mayor Jack Cane's announcement that he is resigning from office, and will serve only until his replacement is seated in November. The three are hanging out in the kitchen eating PB&J sandwiches and watching a continuous loop of the Mayor arriving at the Borough Office, with his wife, Monica. As soon as the press conference ends, and before Malcolm has even submitted his Candidacy papers his name and face appear on screen as the potential front runner in the Mayoral race. Gretchen laughs — the men shoot furtive glances — Gretchen notices — Gretchen ponders — Gretchen lawyers.

"Manuel, why are you here? I mean you are always welcome, but there must be a reason for this unexpected trip," she begins setting her trap as she tidies the kitchen.

"I have a little business to attend," he answers noncommittedly.

"In Lewisburg—Pennsylvania. Malcolm isn't that something, Manuel has business in our little borough. He must have drummed up a little spying opportunity when he came to town to establish paternity of Charlotte."

Manuel shoots eye daggers at Malcolm. "My business is in Washington," he lies.

"Ah, the district of or the state of? I assume you are aware that you're a bit away from both, certainly further from the state than the district. I hear the state of Washington is very beautiful, not that our Nation's capital isn't. Have you ever been to the state of Washington, Manuel? I know you've been to DC, it's where you learned your spying and lying skills—which is why you're in Lewisburg—the spying not the lying, isn't that right?"

Manuel gets up and walks to the elevator. "Talk to your woman, Malcolm. I'll be back."

Gretchen waits until the privacy elevator door closes behind Manuel before turning to Malcolm. In two giant steps he is at Gretchen's side his hand on her baby bump. "Let's go to the game room to talk."

She places her hand on top of his. "Malcolm you're scaring me." He takes her hand, entwines their fingers. They sit opposite one another on their conversation couch.

"Gretchen, there was a woman once."

Gretchen nods. "You told me, but that's all you told me."

"Her name was Sage. I was twenty-five and she was nineteen when we met. If she were here today, she'd probably say that for a short time I saved her from her life as an escort for hire. I didn't save Sage from a damn thing. I took her away from an abusive customer, and I became her only customer. I thought otherwise at the time, but she was my paid girl—then she became significantly more than that. I put her up in a fairytale cottage where she and I had a thing. It's where her former customer found her, and raged her to death."

Gretchen starts to shake. Malcolm takes her hand.

"Her life wasn't the only thing her killer took that night. The bastard took pictures of his brutality. He sends copies to me every year—to remind me of something I will never forget."

The lawyer's mind starts working. A multitude of questions bang through, she settles on one. "Why is Manuel here?"

"I hired him to try to get a lead on the killer, a former private investigator named, Micky Strong." He pauses. He knows this next admission is going to be problematic. "I met Manuel years ago when he handled a hacker-for-hire case for the FBI. The hacker, Stoner Strong, did a couple cyber dives on me, at the request of his uncle. When Manuel was brought in to handle Stoner's investigation back in 2017, he questioned me to see if I knew why Stoner would have hacked me. I didn't tell Manuel what I knew. I'd made a decision at the time of Sage's death that I wouldn't discuss her—ever. Not only did I not say anything to Manuel, but I also didn't tell the detective who questioned me at the time of Sage's murder that she and I had a relationship."

"Obstruction of justice," The lawyer whispers. She turns her cornflowers at him, and lawyers him with a single word, "Continue."

"When Manuel showed up here for the paternity test, we recognized each other. When you and I were at RFI, I showed him the pictures of Sage and asked for his help. I had several meetings with the RFI team – I finally told investigators everything."

Gretchen gets off the couch and paces for several minutes, her hands clenching and unclenching with each step. She stops and addresses Malcolm. "Why? Why are you asking for Manuel's help after all these years?"

He steps toward her and puts his hands on either side of her face. "I need forever, Gretchen, and I'm afraid I'll be robbed of that."

"Again," she whispers.

"What?"

"You're afraid you'll be robbed of that again, like you were robbed of forever with Sage."

"No. What I had with Sage was never about forever. We went into our thing never thinking about a future. Sadly, she was robbed of any future."

Gretchen begins pacing. She comes to a stop in front of a man clearly caught between untold truths and the need to come clean—a man caught between his past and his future.

"Did you love her?"

Malcolm answers too quickly. "I was only with Sage for three months, Gretchen."

She steps back. "There are two problems with your answer, Mr. Price. The first problem is that you didn't answer my question. The second problem is that you and I have only been together for three months." Gretchen's last words catching on a sob. "I'm tired," she says before walking away.

For the next several hours, the very alone man stands at a darkening window staring out at the nothingness around Hufnagle Park waiting for Manuel to exit the privacy elevator. At the sound of the elevator's ping, he makes his way toward the opening door. "She knows," is all he says. He moves down the hallway and stands at the entrance of his bedroom staring at the silent and motionless woman in his bed. He slides next to her, a crushing ache settling deep. He rolls onto his side, hoping she'll find her way into his spoon. She stays curled on her side of the bed.

Deep into the night, Malcolm is pulled from a fractured sleep. He feels her absence and goes in search of the woman he loves beyond all others. He finds her asleep on the couch, the place where hours before, he broke her heart.

I'm losing her — them.

Gretchen wakes Malcolm early. She is already showered and dressed. "May I borrow Magnetite Black; I need to head back to Philly. I've been away from the office far too long."

"Woman, we need to talk. Don't leave."

Gretchen folds her arms across her chest. Malcolm notices her bare ring finger, bolts from bed, and takes her hand, "Woman, please."

She pulls her hand away. "I took the ring off because I don't want anyone at the office seeing it and asking questions that I'm no longer able to answer. It's on the sideboard in the living room, you should put it in your gun case and lock it up. Now, may I please borrow your car?"

"Yes." Malcolm follows Gretchen to the living room and waits silently as the elevator doors close between them.

Gretchen opens Malcolm's Mercedes on the highway loving the feel of the wind that blows free around her. She is surprised that Magnetite Black responds exactly the way Diamond White responded before Cappa Escobar smashed the hell out of it in his attempt to kill her. The memory of Escobar trying to run her down in Malcolm's garage sends a shiver down her spine and springs tears to her eyes. Twenty minutes out of Philly an emotionally wrung Gretchen pulls into a rest stop. She is caught in a fit of racking sobs, shaking limbs, and retching heaves. She is nearly out of the car when Malcolm rushes to her side. He catches her before she hits the ground, lifts her, puts her into the passenger seat of his Land Rover and buckles her in. He runs back to the Mercedes, grabs the keys and Gretchen's stuff, throws it all into the Rover and jams it into gear. He places a call to Manuel, "I'm taking Gretchen to Pennsylvania Hospital, she's unconscious."

On the way Gretchen wakes in a fit of hysteria, she presses her hand tightly against her abdomen, and begins heaving. Malcolm places his arm across her chest to keep her from head butting the dashboard or side window. "Gretchen. Gretchen." The frantic man pulls to a screeching stop at the Emergency Department and carries a semi-conscious Gretchen inside, then stands helplessly as a team of emergency professionals wheel her away. He calls after them, "She's pregnant."

Malcolm takes his cell out to place a call to Gretchen's father, puts it back when he remembers Granger and Faye are on their way to Paris for a month's vacation. Before another thought can pass through his muddled brain, Manuel sprints to the waiting area, "Any news?"

Malcolm shakes his head. "I'm losing her — them."

Manuel puts his hand onto Malcolm's shoulder to comfort the breaking man.

Within an hour's time the men are approached by a nurse, "Mr. Price, Ms. Mitchell is asking for you." Malcolm follows the nurse to a private room. Relief pushes through him when he sees his woman hooked up to a fetal monitor that announces their baby's steady heartbeat. The grateful man moves to the bedside and places a kiss onto Gretchen's head. He sits next to her and takes her hand careful not to disrupt her IV. He drops his head onto their clasped hands.

Gretchen reaches her other hand and places it on to Malcolm's head, "I need to stop running away from you. Whenever I run, something terrible happens. I'm sorry, Malcolm."

"Woman, let's not go there." He scans her face; "you're looking better than the last time I saw you. What did the doctor say?"

"Physically, I'm dehydrated, fatigued and something about my electrolytes being too bright or too dim, I don't know which. Emotionally, I'm a wreck. The doctor thinks I was holding inside everything from the assassination attempt and the shooting. That, in conjunction with the emotional and hormonal changes from the pregnancy, everything just hit all at once and I couldn't control any part of me. They are going to keep me overnight for fluids and observation of 78."

Malcolm touches her belly, "78." A prideful smile takes hold of his face. "78," he says. "That's damned right perfect."

"Do you want to know what we're having?"

Malcolm smiles so wide it's a wonder his face doesn't break, "Yes."

"You'll have to wait," she laughs. "The only thing I know is that our baby is growing strong and will be here sometime after the New Year." Gretchen throws Malcolm one of her million-watt smiles.

Suddenly all is right with his world.

All of it, Manuel.

Manuel is standing in a fifth-floor conference room at the J. Edgar Hoover Building waiting for FICA Director, Stacy Remington, to join him. The former FBI Agent was summoned to Washington—as he knew he would be. He has been waiting nearly an hour, looking out over the hub of the Nation, when the door opens behind him. The Director thumps forward, her outstretched hand motioning to a chair, "Have a seat, and tell me about your interest in Stoner Strong."

"As you know, Stoner was my first case when I worked with the FICA hacker-for-hire division. The cyber hacker had been in FICA's sight for years, and could have been brought in at any time. A decision that pre-dated my tenure was made to let him hack away at relatively inconsequential stuff, and when he went big, the Agency would take him down, and anyone associated with him."

Remington nods.

"I was sent to San Antonio in 2015, and told not to return until I put together a solid case against Stoner. We had him on several charges, and he was eager to whittle down his sentence by giving us information on the people who hired him. The only part of our case where he held his tongue was the Malcolm Price hacking. Stoner said nothing."

There is another nod from the Director.

"Our investigation showed Stoner took his first look at Price when the Spurs were in battle for the 2007 NBA Championship, and did his second dive after the Finals. There were rumors dating back to 2007, that Malcolm Price and Sage Finley had a thing, and that Micky Strong sought revenge against Finley because she left him for Price. During the initial investigation into Finley's murder, 77 acknowledged that he met the paid escort at a Spurs meet and greet, but answered 'no' when he was asked if she was his paid escort." Manuel pauses, then asks Director Remington, "Are you aware of the reference, 77?"

"I don't live under a rock, Manuel, of course I know the reference."

"Yes, ma'am," he smiles.

"Did Mr. Price lie to investigators, or to you?"

"By omission. Sage Finley *was* Malcolm Price's girl. She was not his paid escort—financial documents support that—but he put her up in a cottage to get her out of Tucks projects, and whatever sexual relationship they had didn't begin for weeks after they met. Early in their arrangement, Sage miscarried Micky Strong's kid, so the thing Price and Finley had was centered around keeping her safe." He pauses, not sure how far he should go—not sure how far he's going to have to go.

The Director clears things up for him, "All of it, Manuel."

"Yes, ma'am. Investigators in 2007 had lots on Micky. He was the primary suspect in the killing of Sage Finley. He was a mean drunk, had a history of abusing women, was enraged that Sage left him, and enraged further that she left him for Malcolm Price. He told anyone and everyone that the player and the hooker would pay. The other man in Sage's life—the one everyone protected—was Malcolm Price. Not only was he none of the things Micky Strong was, but he also had an airtight alibi for the night she was killed. For the days leading up to the murder, he was in Lewisburg at a hometown celebration in his honor, and he was flying home around the time of the murder. San Antonio PD pounded the pavement hard for Micky, but when it was learned he'd left San Antonio, the investigation withered and died. If Price had given *something* during any leg of this investigation, we could have looked at accessory before the fact on first-degree murder charges against Stoner, and maybe squeezed him for Micky."

Manuel takes a sip of water, and waits.

After a minute, the Director nods, "Continue."

"Stoner is doing ten years at McKenna Correctional in Waco, Texas. A year or so into his stint, the San Antonio FBI field office got a call from Stoner's then-girlfriend, Chelsea Brady. She said Stoner was a cheating bastard, and she had something the Feds may be interested in having. That something was a key to a San Antonio storage unit originally rented by Micky Strong. The San Antonio Feds took a look around the unit. There wasn't much of Micky's stuff there, certainly nothing that would prove he killed Sage, but there was plenty of stuff to tie Micky to Stoner and Stoner to Malcolm Price. The cyber hacker left a record of payments he received for the work he did for Micky Strong's PI business, including the payments for the Price dives. Stoner got a thousand bucks for the first dive, and five-grand for second dive.

"The records also show a decade worth of five-grand payments to Stoner every July since the murder. I've recently tied those payments to pictures of the gruesome murder scene that Malcolm receives on the anniversary of Sage's murder. We know the killer took the pictures, and we can tie Stoner to sending those pictures. RFI wants to use the mailings and the storage unit payment records as pressure points on Stoner. He's been inside long enough now, that he may be inclined to do a little talking about Micky."

Manuel waits. He knows at some point this conversation is going to get dicey because of Stacy's personal relationship with Granger, and by extension, Gretchen. That point is upon him.

"Why is this coming to light now?" She leans back in her seat, drops her pen on the pad of paper that is still empty. She folds her arms across her chest.

"Malcolm Price is going to declare his candidacy for Mayor of Lewisburg, Pennsylvania, on August 1st with his sights set on the Governor's seat. As soon as he declares, he's going to be put under a microscope, and this time his thing with Sage will become public. Once it does, her murder will be front and center, and it won't take long for the pictures of her brutalized body to be splashed all over the internet. It will help if all fingers point to Micky Strong as the killer of Sage Finley, and not at Malcolm Price." Manuel waits. While he waits, he sees the first crack in Stacy's expression.

"Does Gretchen know about this?"

"She found out yesterday."

"Her response?"

"She almost miscarried their baby."

Stacy pulls a breath. "Does Granger know about the baby?"

"He's in Paris on a month's vacation. When he returns, he will learn that Gretchen and Malcolm are engaged, are expecting a baby, and he's running for public office. I'm unsure how or when Granger will learn about the Sage Finley matter." Manuel waits.

Stacy shifts in her seat, and picks up her pen. She taps in once on the table. "Let's have RFI take point on this. That's a basketball reference, a specific one related to 77, in case you are unaware."

Manuel smiles big, "Yes, ma'am."

"I'll want my people in the room when you talk to Stoner Strong, but you handle the case through RFI. As for Granger, I won't need to discuss this with him, unless and until I bring the case back to J. Edgar."

Stacy Remington gets up and leaves the room without further ado.

I took a knee for her.

Malcolm settles Gretchen in the game room before heading out. "I'll be back mid-afternoon. Please rest, and don't marinate, Woman. We'll talk everything out tonight. Manuel is in the guest suite if you need him." Malcolm simultaneously kisses the top of Gretchen's head and pats their baby bump. "Take care of Mommy, 78." He leaves 275 Market Street and heads to his old stomping grounds. He pulls his Land Rover to a stop at his childhood home and takes the four front steps all at once, "Mama Girl, you ready to go?" he hollers as the screen door slams closed behind him.

"Keep your pants on Malcolm, I'm coming, and you're early," Bertha Price hollers back. Mama Girl has said nearly the same words to her boy his entire life. She says many things over and over making sure the important stuff sticks—like knowing they are descendants of a man who was brought to the shores of Savannah on a slave ship and sold alongside food and clothes. She made sure Malcolm understood the importance of working hard, earning a fair wage, and banking whatever isn't needed "For a roof over, and food on". She let him know she found herself pregnant at seventeen and did the best she could to have her child and raise him tall and proud. The one thing Bertha King Price didn't tell her son is the most important thing of all—the name of his father. The obedient child that he was and respectful man that he is accepts what his Mama Girl shared. Malcolm has never asked for more and has resisted finding out for himself.

It has been weeks since Malcolm spent any measurable amount of time with his mother. During those weeks so much has happened to him, but mostly to the woman he loves. Gretchen was almost killed by a hired assassin; was taken into protective custody at his penthouse; participated in a sting operation to capture the hitman who had a 'don't stop' order against her; and helped unite a father and his infant daughter. Now that things have settled a bit, there is so much more he needs to tell his Mama Girl.

Bertha approaches her son with wide arms, "I've missed you boy. Tell me about your woman."

Malcolm smiles wide. "I took a knee for her."

Bertha slaps her hand on her thigh, "And did she take a knee for you, son?"

"Sure did, Mama Girl."

Malcolm steps in for an embrace, but pulls short when he sees the expression on her face. "Something bothering you, Mama Girl?"

"Same thing that's bothering you, son. Talk to me, boy."

Malcolm sits with his mother and says the one word that sets his Mama Girl's head to nodding and shaking.

"Sage."

Mama Girl places her hand on her son's knee. "She's part of you, Malcolm, it's time to start dealing with her."

He gets up, finds the nearest wall, leans back and lowers his head. "I told Gretchen about Sage last night."

"Is she still on her knee for you, boy?"

Malcolm shakes his head. "Mama Girl, Gretchen is having my baby and she almost lost it last night from the pain of it all."

Mama Girl waits for her son to gather himself then sets him straight. "Almost, is the important word here, boy. You tender your woman through this and don't ever keep secrets again." The woman has her say then gets up and walks to the door, "Get a move on," she says before the screen door slams closed behind her.

275

Gretchen is sitting on the couch mindlessly watching MSNBC when Manuel enters the game room from the guest suite. He walks to her and places a kiss on top of her head, "Gave us a scare, Gretchen. How are you feeling?"

She places her hand on her belly, "**We**, are feeling fine. Didn't hear you come in last night, was it a late one?"

"Yeah. Didn't want to disturb you, so I came up from the back alley."

Gretchen smiles. "How was your trip to Washington, the district of, not the state of," she smiles again.

Manuel taps her feet; she lifts them then drops them onto his lap when he sits. "You and I aren't going to talk about this without Malcolm, I hope you understand," Manuel says with a note of finality.

"Understood. Why don't you tell me about Muriel and Charlotte. How are they doing?"

"Muriel, and the rest of The Compound team, is caring for and fussing over Charlotte. Muriel says she is a perfect little baby. I'm a happy man, Gretchen." His couch mate throws him a look. "What?" he asks with a tone.

Gretchen shrugs a shoulder, "I'm admitting, for the record, that I don't know you all that well, but I've seen genuine moments of happiness in you, and this," she waves her hand in his direction, "is not reflective of a happy Manuel."

"It's just been a lot to take in."

"Yes, well, perhaps that's it, but..." She pauses and waits for an invitation to discuss this particular topic further. She receives none, so she alters their conversational tract, "I'm sorry our business has taken you away from Muriel and Charlotte. When do you think you can head back?"

Manuel trenches *that* smile. "No need to be wily, Gretchen, we're not talking until Malcolm gets home." He smiles again, lifts her legs off his lap, places them gently onto the couch, and heads to the door, "I'm starved, do you need anything?"

"Nope, I'm good and apparently unsuccessful in the wily department this morning," she calls after him.

Mama Girl suggests a post-dialysis trip to Malcolm's place so she can get some lovin' from Gretchen. When the mother and son enter the game room they find two people in a heated backgammon game, with the blonde player's draughts poised for a quick bear off, a move sure to crush her opponent. The spectators stay quiet until their woman whops the good-natured loser. A victorious Gretchen hops from the couch when she sees there are guests. "Mama Girl," she squeals.

"You sit, Woman." Mama Girl wraps Gretchen tight, "I heard there was an almost scare with my grandbaby. There'll be no more of that. I set your man straight about untruths and half-truths and there will be no more of that, either."

Gretchen eyes her man who has clearly had an earful from his Mama Girl. "And you Gretchen, when your man has a piece to say you listen and think before you run. And if running is what you're gonna do, then so be it. Now, let me see the ring of intentions."

Everyone looks at Gretchen's naked finger. "I...I took it off...for safe keeping," Gretchen tries.

"I'd say you took it off for some safe thinking. Can't say as I blame you, this Sage business has been buried too long. Well, it's been dug up now. Best work it through." Mama Girl turns to Manuel, "You have a woman?"

"Yes, ma'am," Manuel says. "Sort of," he adds.

"Well, can't say I can help you figure out if you've got a woman, but I can set you straight on how to keep one. Sit back down, you'll learn some today, boy."

Mama Girl sets everyone straight on truth telling and men who think they know best how to care for their women, then she sends the men away. She sits next to Gretchen and puts a hand on the expectant woman's knee. "Ask the burning questions, Gretchen, you won't rest a lick until you do. Fair warning, I deal in full-truth, so only ask what you can handle."

Gretchen pulls a long cleansing breath. "Tell me about Sage, please."

"Never met the girl, but I knew her deep." The woman's eyes set tight on Gretchen's, making sure her son's woman **hears** her meanings and not just her words. "Sage was like me when she landed in Malcolm's sight—pregnant, alone, and doing what she needed to do to survive. Sad truths, Gretchen, some women get beaten down by a man's clenched fist, others by a man's promises that can never be met. Matters little for the woman who struggles to survive after her beating, especially if she is surviving for two. Women do what **needs** to be done, using what they have." Mama Girl sighs then throws her head high having told her full-truth.

Gretchen puts her hand on top of Mama Girls and waits.

"Sage was nineteen when she met my boy. That night, he saw things in her that called him to help. He had her quit the business, helped get her momma's ashes from the projects where she was barely surviving, and put her up in a little cottage for himself. Can't say I approve. Can't say I can judge. After the girl miscarried her abuser's child, she saw some light ahead. She was preparing for her GED, and Malcolm was setting her up in college. The girl loved flowers and wanted to learn how to grow them."

Mama Girl pauses and shakes her head slowly, "You've heard how Sage died, so there's no need in bringing that ugliness into this conversation. Malcolm buried that girl and her momma side by side at his ranch in Texas."

Gretchen wipes tears from her cheeks and accepts the squeeze of her hand from Mama Girl. Then she sets about asking her burning question, "Did Malcolm love her? I asked him, but he didn't answer."

"He loved her right fine for what she was to him. My son is a man of compassion, far too often confused with feelings of the heart. Don't really know all of his feelings for Sage, but I do know he's never been in 'surrendering love' until you."

Gretchen falls apart at Mama Girl's words. After a bit, Malcolm's mother has her say for Gretchen, "The next time you put my son's ring of intentions on your finger, you leave it on, and you stay put and fight it out with your man. You keep running—you might look back and find he's not chasing."

"Yes, ma'am," Gretchen says through her tears.

Mama Girl pats Gretchen's knee before rising from the couch. "I'm sending my son in while I talk to that other fine looking man a bit."

Gretchen is moving to the game room door when Malcolm walks in. "Where you going, Woman?"

She runs her fingers through Malcolm's scruff, "I'll be waiting for you in the bedroom. When you get back from taking Mama Girl home, I hope you'll join me for a shower."

"No need to wait. Manuel took Mama Girl home. She said you and I need to unwind some," Malcolm smiles wide.

"And?" Gretchen smiles wide.

"And I do what Mama Girl says." Malcolm offers his gigantic hand to Gretchen. She accepts it.

Malcolm and Gretchen hunger one another with urgent touches and searing kisses. Rapid panting and guttural moans fill the space around them. Malcolm lifts Gretchen and stands her on a built-in shower seat and kneels down. She holds onto his shoulders as he enjoys her and leaves her trembling. He carries his spent woman to his bed, lays next to her, his want desperate. "Are we good Gretchen? Can I press you?" She nods. He supports his weight over her and gentles in and in and in until he feels her tighten and hears and feels her release of satisfaction. Malcolm leaves everything he has deep in his woman. When they are sufficiently unwound, he rests her head on his chest, takes her hand and slips his ring back onto her finger.

"Forever, Gretchen."

"Forever, Malcolm."

Before and after.

Manuel arrived back at The Compound late from his trip to Lewisburg having been set straight on a few things by Mama Girl. He spent the night camped out on the couch, so as not to disturb Muriel and Charlotte. That. Is. Bullshit. He stayed on the couch because Mama Girl's words cut deep. They banged the shit out of him on the trip home, and all through the night. They are still banging hard as he makes his way across The Compound grounds…

"What's the truth about the woman who's sharing your bed, Manuel?"

He shook his head, "Muriel needs a place to stay. I need help with Charlotte. I guess you could say we're at a mutual place of needing each other."

"Sounds like an awful place to be."

After avoiding a night with the woman he needs, Manuel thinks about the woman he wants, for a split second – then he admonishes himself… "Get Leavy out of your head!"

"What?" Joy asks as she passes him on her way to a waiting transport vehicle, an overnight bag in hand.

"Nothing. Just preparing for my meeting."

"Uh huh," she laughs. "See you when we get back."

"Back?"

"From London," she shoots him a 'duh' look.

"Shit. London. Right. London." He continues setting himself straight… "Get your shit together!"

"What?" Annie asks as she passes him on her way to the firing range.

"Nothing. Just preparing for my meeting."

"Uh huh," she smirks.

"Fuck. What the fuck is wrong with me?" he demands.

"Ah, the question that plagues all men," Rocco says as he passes his son on the way to the waiting transport vehicle. "Perhaps you will be of freer heart and mind upon my return."

"Doubtful."

"Si," Rocco laughs.

A team of three is waiting in the office for Manuel. He pushes into the cramped space, and throws a file onto the desk.

"Nice of you to join us," Fred quips.

He ignores the quip. "Let's get up to speed on the Malcolm Price case."

"We're all up to speed. Call girl. Two-bit PI. Pro-athlete. Girl is murdered. PI books out of town. Athlete obstructs initial investigation. You get a hacker-for-hire case. You tell Malcolm the hacker did two jobs on him in 2007. Malcolm obstructs your investigation. Hacker is doing a dime at McKenna Correctional Facility in Waco for cyber related shit. He could be doing more. That's how far up to speed we…"

"Jackass." Manuel tosses the envelope of pictures of a hacked Sage Finley onto the desk, they scatter across.

"What the fuck. A heads up would've been nice, jackass," Mike says as he gathers the gruesome pics, takes a flip through and passes them to Fred, "Seen them," he offers them to Leavy, she raises her hand in refusal.

"Well **that** got our attention. Having a bad morning, Manuel?" Fred pushes. "Because you're sure turning my morning to shit. Care to explain?"

"Dealing with some personal shit, that I should have left at the door. Won't happen again." He eye-checks his team, one by one they nod. He moves on after a second look at Leavy. "Okay, San Antonio FBI field office recently got their hands on a key to Micky Strong's storage facility…"

Fred interrupts, his deep dimpling smile already on his face. "Tell me the Feds found something."

Manuel matches Fred's smile with one of his own. "Stoner's financials — a detailed record of monies received for jobs done. He got a grand for the full hack on Price, and an additional five-grand for the recon dive. That's the dive we're interested in, it's how we are going to press Stoner and get Micky."

"On the edge of our seats, Manuel." Fred pushes.

"Stoner got departing and returning flight information for Malcolm, and an itinerary for a hometown celebration in Lewisburg that he'd be attending. The intel confirmed Price would be gone from August 1 until August 5, the day Sage was murdered. The payment connects Stoner to the intel, which means the hacker-for-hire has a BIG problem. Wendell 'Stoner' Strong told Micky when Malcolm was going out of town and how long he'd be gone. He provided a window of opportunity for the murderer of Sage Finley. That translates to Stoner Strong being charged as an accessory before the fact in a first-degree murder case."

"Good. The douchebag deserves to go down for his part in all of this," Leavy scoffs.

"No argument," Manuel smiles, "but there's more. On or about the anniversary of Sage Finley's murder, a set of pictures of the brutalized young woman is sent to Malcolm Price – a sort of anniversary gift. Stoner's books reflect an annual payment of five-grand coming in around that same time period. The person who took those pictures is the person who was with Sage as she lay dying. We know the murdering son-of-a-bitch is Micky Strong. We know the person who sends those pictures is

Stoner Strong – that makes him an accessory after the fact. Our plan: convince Stoner we are filing murder charges against Micky Strong in absentia, and since Micky isn't around to face the charges, the person going down for Sage Finley is the asshole currently sitting his ass in jail."

Manuel gives his associates a minute to toss the information around and ask questions. It's a professional courtesy, one that isn't needed with this group.

"Okay, this is what I want. Leavy, go deep on Stoner Strong. Get all the normal background stuff. Pay attention to his bank accounts, look for a trail for the annual $5,000 payments. Maybe we can match deposits to the incoming payments. If we're lucky, maybe get a hit on a wire transfer for the funds. Also, check his travel history see if he goes out of town in July, maybe he picks up his payment from Micky. Then do a dive on Garden of Eve, the escort service, especially on its owner Eve Lappier. See if you can get a roster of Eve's girls. Malcolm said Micky replaced Sage with a buxom blonde during the 2007 Finals, maybe we can find her and talk to her. Then get anything you can on Micky Strong. He probably changed his name and got fake documents before leaving San Antonio, so look for people in the area who provide that type of service. Fred, Mike and I are hitting the road for a little one on one conversations with people in San Antonio and Wyldwood. We'll save the big conversation with Stoner Strong until the end."

Halifax to London

The RFI jet is full of passengers — that is to say the jet is full of personalities. In one seat, there is Rocco Fiancetti aka Alistair Duff, a former Senior Special Operative with the Secret Intelligence Service of the U.K. in a branch commonly known as MI6. Sitting across from him is Joy Fiancetti aka DOA, a former Special Agent with the Federal Bureau of Investigations of the U.S. in a branch commonly known as FICA.

The SSO of the SIS aka MI6 is taking the SA of the FBI aka FICA to London to meet with the IG of the SIS and the AIG of MI6. In other words — in full words, Rocco is taking Joy to London to meet his former boss, Mick Bentley and his former colleague, Andria Covington. "Tell me about Inspector General Bentley."

"Ah. Mick is of a doppelganger to George Clooney." Rocco studies his woman – there is no response to that bit of news. No sigh, no moan, no blush, no flush—which, for the record is unusual. Most women sigh, moan, blush and flush, in that order, at the mere mention of Mick Bentley and of his doppelganger. Rocco smiles and continues. "It took decades, but Mick has settled into his good looks, and wears the creases of life well. His handsomeness benefitted him and hindered him as a spy."

"I can imagine." Mrs. Fiancetti smiles wickedly.

"There is a message in your smile, Gia. A devilish one."

"I'm a cyber huntress. I have seen pictures of Mick Bentley. And for the record, when you studied me earlier and saw nothing, please know this, just because you did not see me swoon, does not mean I did not swoon. I am a spy, Rocco. I don't have a tell."

"You are mistaken, Gia. The drum of your fingers is your tell."

Joy smiles wickedly, "Not my only tell."

"Ah. Perhaps a panty inspection is of warrant."

"Inspect away Mr. Fiancetti."

She did as she was told.

Mr. and Mrs. Granger Mitchell are wrapped in one another's arms, admiring their shiny new wedding bands. They are in a magnificent bed, in a luxurious suite, across the way from the Eiffel Tower. So in love are they, so captivated by one another, that they have yet to cast an eye on the iconic tower. Still…

"Granger."

"Mmmmm."

"Your phone is ringing."

"Mmmmm."

"You should get it. It might be Gretchen."

"Uh huh," he mumbles into a kiss upon her nestled head.

The wife nudges. The husband reluctantly answers the call. "It's late, Gretchen."

"Yes, Daddy, but I need…"

Granger hears nothing more. He sits up wondering if the call has ended when sounds of sobs find his ear. "Gretchen are you crying?" He is met with silence. "Gretchen, is Malcolm with you?" Sobs. "Gretchen give Malcolm the phone." He shrugs his shoulder in answer to Faye's questioning look. "Malcolm. What is this call about?"

"I'm sorry for the interruption, Granger, but there are some things going on in Gretchen's life, in our life, that she wants to share. She's a bit overcome at the moment, so I will speak for her."

"Go on," Granger says.

"Gretchen has accepted my proposal of marriage, and she is pregnant with our baby. Those two events are connected only by timing. I love your daughter passionately and intended to propose before she surprised me about the baby. I had hoped to ask your permission for Gretchen's hand in marriage, but there are other things going on that prevented that from happening."

"Go on," Granger says.

"Mayor of Lewisburg, Jack Cane, announced he is retiring due to illness. My plan is to file Intent for Candidacy papers on August 1st. There is an issue from my past that needs to be resolved before I declare my intentions. I have enlisted the services of RFI to help with this matter. Unless this situation is resolved before August 1st, I will be unable to seek the office of Mayor."

"Sage Finley?" Granger offers.

"Yes."

"Tell Gretchen we are on our way home. And Malcolm, congratulations on the engagement, the baby, and your political future."

Gretchen, who had her cheek pressed against Malcolm's to ensure she could hear the conversation between her two men, pulls back when the call ends. She dives headfirst into a word mash. "Granger Mitchell knows about Sage Finley? Let's see, who ever could have told him? Stacy Remington perhaps, or did Granger Mitchell have you 'looked' at. And if he had you 'looked' at why didn't he tell me about Sage? I am, after all, the one involved with you. Ooooo, I wonder if he has information that can help us find Micky Strong." Gretchen stops her rant when she sees the hooded eyes and pinched lips of her man.

"Woman, there is no **us** when it comes to Micky Strong. Manuel is handling this."

Gretchen shrugs.

"Gretchen," Malcolm growls.

"All right, all right," she concedes with fingers crossed behind her back. For the record, that's going to be her defense when Malcolm calls her out on the snooping **she is going to do**. She pushes that unpleasantness aside, and focuses on what is happening at that moment. The hopeful future Mrs. Mayor, sits across from Malcolm watching him complete the Intent papers. Although its weeks from August 1st he begins talking about his campaign.

"Abigail Forrester called and offered her services as my Campaign manager, 'should I consider making my candidacy official'. Have any thoughts on Ms. Forrester's offer?"

"I don't know anything about Abigail personally, but from a political standpoint you can't get a better strategist. She ran Jack Cane's campaign, and she has a long record with winners throughout the Keystone State," Gretchen opines.

"Agreed. If I hire her, I'll need to tell her about Sage. I'd like to wait to see if Manuel gets a lead on Micky before heading down that road." Malcolm gets up from his desk and approaches Gretchen, "Maybe the timing isn't right for this."

Gretchen gently shakes her head. "You won't know if the timing is right or wrong until after the fact. You want this and the opportunity to have this is now. As for the real issues regarding time, it's time for me to go to bed. You coming with?" Gretchen asks on a yawn.

"In a few." He walks Gretchen to their bedroom, heads back to the game room, takes his customary place against a wall, and lets Sage take her place inside his head…

He entered the meet and greet. He eyed the girl through a throng of revelers, was slow getting to her, "Malcolm Price," he said with a wide smile.

"Sage Finley," she said with the dip of her head. "The game was a bit slow tonight, Mr. Price." She flashed a wide toothy smile.

He laughed.

~

He answered on the fifth ring. "Price."

"Mr. Price, this is Sage Finley, I met you this evening."

"What can I do for you, Sage?"

"I need a ride home."

"Are you alone?"

"Yes."

"Where are you?"

"Pembroke Hotel on…"

"I know the place," Malcolm interrupted. "Room number?"

"212."

"Stay inside. I'll be there in twenty minutes. Don't let him back in." Malcolm knocked on the hotel room door fifteen minutes later. "It's 77."

Sage opened the door.

The MAN was pushed back by her beauty, angered by other things.

Sage was dressed in the same outfit as earlier in the evening, but she'd been accessorized with a few new things—a red grab mark on her bicep and a handprint across her face.

"Get your things," he said through clenched teeth.

She wagged her purse toward him, "This is it."

The unsmiling man took her hand and lead her out of the fleabag hotel and to his Mercedes parked around the corner. He opened her door then headed to his. As he climbed in, he saw Micky Strong heading back inside the hotel.

The young woman saw him too. She pushed low into her seat and shivered.

"Where to, Sage?" He started the Mercedes and pulled out of the parking lot.

"Tucks," was all she said. It's all she needed to say.

Malcolm eyed her. "You live in the projects? Those projects? Pretty rough place. You live there alone?"

"I do now that Momma died." Sage turned to look out the side window.

Malcolm noticed the sudden tears that wet Sage's eyes as she turned away. He picked up his cell and pressed a number, "Hey, Sammi, I need a place near the ranch."

"For tonight?" the woman asked.

"Indefinitely," he replied and hung up.

"You missed the turnoff to Tucks, Mr. Price."

"We're going to dinner, first."

~

Malcolm pulled to a stop and opened his door to get out. Sage opened her door to get out.

"Shut the door, Sage."

She did as she was told.

The tall, powerful man rounded the Benz and opened the passenger door. He offered the young woman his gigantic hand; she slipped hers in and let him help her out. He placed his hand to the small of her back and lead her inside a roadside burger joint—somewhere between San Antonio and Austin. He grabbed a booth in the back.

"You come here a lot," Sage said, barely above a whisper.

"It's between where I work and where I live."

The wary young woman took a look around, "Mr. Price, I need to get back to San Antonio and check in with the service."

He handed her his cell phone. "Call them. Tell them you quit."

Sage dropped the fork she'd been nervously twirling. "I can't quit," she says on an exhaled laugh.

Malcolm slid his phone toward her. "Call."

Sage reached for his cell, halted when she saw the tremble in her hand. She looked at her non-paying escort for reassurance.

He nodded. "Call."

The working girl picked up the phone, put it back on the table when Malcolm received a call

"Sammi, what have you got?" He listened. "Sounds good. Rent it, put everything in your name, I don't want her or me traceable. Thanks, Sammi."

He turned his attention to Sage. "You have a new place to live. Do you need anything from Tucks?"

"Mr. Price, could you please explain what's going on?"

"You are out of the business and it's Malcolm."
He smiled w.i.d.e. hoping to take the edge off.

"Am I going to be your personal escort?" she
asked tentatively.

"Maybe later. Right now, you need to be away
from the dick."

Sage reflexively rubbed her bicep and
nodded. "I need Momma's ashes from Tucks."

"I'll have someone take you when I'm at the
Center tomorrow." He tapped his phone. "Make
the call."

She did as she was told.

~

Malcolm leaned against a counter his feet
crossed at the ankles, "How old are you?"

"Nineteen."

"Come here. I want to taste you."

Sage walked the few steps to him, placed
a foot on either side of his crossed feet, and
pressed against him. His excitement was long
and hard along her belly. He skipped his
fingertips across her bangs, then ran his hand
the length of her long hair before cupping the
back of her head. He kissed her long and deep,
groaned long and deep. "I want to do things with
you, Sage, but you're in no condition, and there are
things about this arrangement you need to understand.
You are not my whore. You have a say in what we do
if we do. When you want out, you're out. There isn't a
fairytale ending in this fairytale cottage. If you fall in

love, you will end up being hurt. Think about it when I'm gone."

He pushed himself to a full stand causing Sage to pull away. He fingered her bangs and ran his hand the full length of her silky strands before leaving a kiss on her cheek. He walked to the door calling over his shoulder, "Lock the door, and put on security."

She did as she was told.

"Damn fool, thinking I did Sage any better than Micky did." The self-castigating man spends a fitful night on the game room couch.

Paris to Philadelphia

Mr. and Mrs. Granger Mitchell canoodle a bit in their first-class seats on an unplanned early return flight to the States. "Faye," a kiss upon her temple, a whispered something against her cheek, "I wish we could have stayed longer," a kiss upon the corner of her lips, "but we'll always have Paris."

The missus laughs, "Oh, Granger, that was a perfect imitation of Humphrey Bogart."

The besotted man takes an eyeful, and whispers on his way for another kiss, "Here's looking at you, kid."

"Oh Bogie," she swoons.

Don't push me on this.

Researcher Randy smiles wide when he sees Gretchen's name on his caller ID. "Yo, Miss Mitchell, it's been a while. How's 77?"

Gretchen sighs – loudly, "We're fine, thanks for asking. Listen, Randy, I was supposed to come into the office, but I've got some things going on in Lewisburg. I'd like you to gather a few things and bring them to Malcolm's place. The list is long, so I'll email it to you. And I'm going to need you to work with me for a few days, so pack the best computer system you have for deep cyber diving, and pack an overnight bag because you're staying at 77's."

"Holy shit, I mean, yes, of course, Miss Mitchell. I'll be there later today, tell 77 to expect me."

Gretchen laughs, "Will do."

Malcolm joins Gretchen in the kitchen. "Who are you bothering this early in the morning, Woman?"

"Researcher Randy. He's gathering some stuff for me. I hope you don't mind if we work from here for a few days."

"Don't mind."

"Even if Randy stays a couple nights?"

"Even if," Malcolm says, as he heads out for a run. A quick five miles and a shower later, and he's off to get Mama Girl for her dialysis treatment.

Researcher Randy arrives a little after noon, offers a "Yo, 77, I'm here!" as he steps off the privacy elevator.

"I'm here, too," Gretchen laughs. "Put our stuff on the coffee table. Let's have some lunch before jumping in." As Gretchen flits, Randy eyes the R.I.N.G. on T.H.E. finger. His glances go without comment or question. She knows he wants to comment and question. She pushes her lunch plate away, and puts on her serious face, "Everything I am about to say to you is beyond confidential, Randy. I know I have your loyalties, but I need you to cover 77's ass, too."

Randy breaks a wide smile, "Perfectly honest, Miss Mitchell, my loyalties to 77 are solid. Since you're his woman and my boss, I've got your back, too."

"Good to know. So this is what is going on. Malcolm and I are engaged. Malcolm and I are expecting a baby. Malcolm is running for Mayor of Lewisburg and will announce his candidacy on August 1st. You and I are going to hack into Malcolm's past."

Randy's smile widens with each bit of information—until there's mention of hacking 77. "Due respect, Miss Mitchell, I can't imagine

Malcolm Price, you know, 6'5", built like Batman with the strength of the Hulk, Malcolm Price, is going to take kindly to you messing in his business. And while I enjoy being invited into 77's lair, it is not my desire to end my days here. You're my boss, Miss Mitchell, so you have me over a barrel. That said, I'm hoping you accept that my intentions are solid when I ask you if you are out of your ever-loving mind?"

Gretchen laughs big. "I appreciate your concern. Go get settled while I clean the kitchen.

Randy stores his gear, sets his computer system in the guest suite, then heads back to the kitchen. When he rounds the corner from the game room, he runs face to chest into Malcolm, and freezes.

"Hey, kid." Malcolm goes to tap Randy on the shoulder and Randy flinches.

Malcolm shoots a look and a laugh at Gretchen, "What's up with the kid?"

Gretchen shrugs and throws Randy a look.

Randy shrugs and throws a look of his own.

Malcolm catches it all, "Randy, what did my woman ask you to do?"

Randy shoots a pleading look to Gretchen. She ignores it.

"Kid," Malcolm growls.

"She'll fire me," Randy groans.

"I'll kill you," Malcolm threatens.

"She wants me to hack you. Sorry, Miss Mitchell, I'll just get my things from the guest suite and go pick up my last paycheck." Randy turns to leave.

"Go to the suite. Do not pack," Malcolm growls. Malcolm catches up to Gretchen in the bedroom in three giant ass steps, "Woman," he points to the bed, "sit."

Gretchen stands her ground. He stares her down. She crosses her arms over her chest. He stares her down. She taps her toes. He stares her down. She walks across the room and sits on the bed. He kneels in front of her and takes her hands. "Gretchen, let Manuel handle this. If you need to know about Sage, we'll talk. I have never demanded anything from you before, Gretchen, but I am **telling you** to leave this alone. I'm not asking you. Don't push me on this, Woman." Malcolm leaves the room and the apartment.

Gretchen steams a bit then heads to the guest room and knocks on the door. She opens it a crack and finds Randy sitting on the edge of the bed just as she'd been doing only moments before. "May I come in," she asks softly.

Randy gets up and starts to speak. Gretchen cuts him off, "I shouldn't have put you between Malcolm and me, I'm sorry, Randy."

"I'm not fired?" He asks expectantly.

"Of course not. Come, on Turncoat, we've got work to do. Non-77 related work."

Researcher Randy smiles wide and follows her to the living room, he sits on the floor as Gretchen roams the space. He notices that she checks the wall clock every few minutes. "77 will be back, Miss Mitchell," he reassures her.

"I shouldn't have forced him to leave," she softly admits.

"Damned straight, but shit happens."

Gretchen paces herself to the bank of windows, and watches for her man.

Malcolm returns after dark. He hears the shower off the master bedroom running. Before heading there, he goes in search of Researcher Randy. He finds him in the game room watching ESPN.

"She didn't fire you?" Malcolm asks with a smile.

"No, she apologized," Randy shrugs.

Malcolm's smile widens. He reaches into his pocket, tosses Randy a $100 bill and a set of keys to the back entrance. "Step out of 275 for a while. When you come back, use the back entrance, it leads directly to the guest suite. Be home by midnight."

Randy nods and on his way past Malcolm he says, "Congratulations on the engagement and the baby."

Malcolm taps Randy on the shoulder—this time the kid doesn't flinch.

The man of 275 finds his woman sitting on the shower floor, her knees bent, her arms wrapped tight around them, and her forehead resting on top.

"Woman, why are you sitting on the floor when there's a built-in seat right there?"

Gretchen talks into her bent knees. "That's where you gentle me, it didn't feel right sitting there."

Malcolm holds his laugh, "Woman, you seem a bit broken. You ready to be fixed?"

Gretchen nods. Malcolm strips and enters her sad space. When he's gentled her a bit he enters her happy place.

What Abigail wants.

Benton Brettenvue, founder and CEO of The Brettenvue Group, a lobbying firm in Philadelphia, Pennsylvania, is in a closed-door meeting with his mistress, Abigail Forrester.

"I don't like coming here, Benton."

"Don't worry, Celia is out of town."

"I don't give a rat's ass about your wife. It's the fucking FBI knocking on your door *and* my door that freaks me out. Next time you want to introduce me to some international crime lord, don't."

Benton scoffs, "There isn't going to be a next time. Antonio Alvarez is behind bars—Cappa Escobar is dead—The Realm is disbanded—and Dominique is serving a life sentence. The FBI hasn't been able to prove my involvement with any of the shit that's gone down. I am free and clear, and so are you."

"What about Roland Gaffney?"

"What about him," Benton stops his roaming and stares at Abigail.

She stares back. "The former Director of FICA is sitting in a Federal prison because of his association with The Realm. I'm sure he's expecting help from someone — that means there is someone — someone powerful enough to make sure Gaffney doesn't sing."

"Don't know – don't want to know, Abigail."

"Don't bother with the bullshit, Benton. You know you're up to your ass in shit and it has everything to do with The Realm."

He drills her with his eyes, snaps out a course reversal, **"The only thing I want to know is whether Malcolm Price is going to ask you to be his campaign manager."** As he makes his way to his office bar, he cools a bit, then holds up a bottle in Abigail's direction, "Share a drink?"

"No."

"Suit yourself." He pours himself three fingers of his favorite single-malt whiskey, pulls a sip and continues. "Has the next mayor of Lewisburg called you, yet?"

"He will," Abigail says confidently. "Now that his face is above the fold in newspapers across the county as the front runner in a race he hasn't even entered, he's going to want the best person to handle his campaign. I'm the best."

"**You** dropped his name to the Press," Benton surmises.

Abigail smiles.

"What about the soon-to-be former Mayor Jack Cane? Any pushback from him, now that you've forced him out of office?" he asks before draining his drink.

Abigail brushes imaginary lint from her pant leg, "Jack Cane knows what will happen if he says Word One — the pictures I have of him will be made public. He may not be ill now, but he will be if his holier than thou and richer than God wife and their Ivy-league offspring get wind of Mr. Kinky-Pants…" Abigail raises her hand to halt the conversation, takes hold of her briefcase, reaches in and pulls out her ringing cell. Her grin spreads from ear to ear, "It's Malcolm Price." She answers the call, "Mr. Price, may I call you back in ten minutes, I'm just finishing a meeting … Great. Thanks." Abigail gathers her things and glares at Benton, "I don't want you crawling on top of me drunk, so either dry up or don't come over tonight," she says as the door to Benton's office closes behind her.

"Bitch," he calls after her.

Abigail laughs off the comment, and steps inside the corporate elevator. When the doors close and she catches her reflection in the highly polished brass door, she is instantly transported back to Hell—her Hell.

"You aren't pretty yet, Abigail, but one day, perhaps," her grandmother would say as they sat on the family porch in Scranton, Pennsylvania. "But don't worry yourself, mining men don't much care what a woman looks like, so long as she can cook a meal, pack a lunch, and take to their bed."

Abigail decided then and there she would rather eat her weight in anthracite coal than stay in Scranton. And once she got out, she vowed she'd never return. Now that she's earned her cred in the political arena, she knows she'll never have to. That doesn't mean her Scranton roots don't find their way in from time to time.

"Interesting. I'd say your look is interesting."

The bang of her grandma's words causes Abigail to take one last look at her reflection inside the posh elevator, "Oval face, auburn hair that tends to frizz, standard-fare blue eyes, nice high cheekbones, lips are a little pinched, though." She checks her attire, "Black pantsuit, yellow button-down blouse, black pumps. Okay, so I come up a bit short in the looks department, but my grit is legendary. And **that** is what will get me everything I want."

And what Abigail wants is to bring
Malcolm Price to his knees.

275 Market Street
The political strategist is smiling broadly when she exits the privacy elevator into the living room of 275 Market Street. "Abigail Forrester," she says as she extends her hand in introduction to Malcolm and then to Gretchen who are waiting inside. "I hope you don't mind if I gush over this space for a minute. This is such a beautiful rehab, and in my opinion, the focal piece of all

the other revitalization projects that are being done in this area."

Gretchen smiles and takes Abigail on a tour while Malcolm heads to his office. A half-hour later, the ladies join him.

"Great use of the space, Mr. Price. It's very beautiful."

"Malcolm," he encourages.

Abigail nods as she walks the office space looking at the array of civic awards and plaques. She stops at the key to the borough of Lewisburg, "You know, you could be using that key to open your office—if you are in the race, **and** if you are smart enough to hire me to run your campaign."

"Have a seat, Abigail," Malcolm says.

Philadelphia

Benton Brettenvue is mostly sober when he climbs onto Abigail Forrester later that night.

"Ease up, Benton, I'm not a trampoline, never mind, get off," she hisses. The put-upon, and pumped-upon woman, pushes out of bed and pulls on a robe, "Get dressed and meet me in the kitchen."

Benton saunters down many minutes later. "If you weren't going to let me pound your pussy, you should have let me stay drunk."

"Dry up. The stakes just got high. I'm Malcolm Price's campaign manager. The official announcement will be made when he files his

Intent papers on August 1st. That will put me in close proximity and give me plenty of time behind the scenes to find something to fuck up his run. I didn't go to all the trouble of getting Jack Cane out of the Mayor's office, so Malcolm Price could walk in. I need Topher Griffin in the mayor's seat, and he will be once I make Malcolm Price unelectable."

Damned arrogance.

The borough of Lewisburg is part of Union County in Central Pennsylvania. It is located on the West Branch of the Susquehanna River, and is home to 6,200 residents. The demographics of the borough is approximately ninety percent white, and the per capital income is slightly north of $42,000. Malcolm Price knows personally that there are too many people living below the poverty level in The Burg. He also knows the most heralded thing in the borough is its award-winning public-school system, and highly regarded Bucknell University—both of which Malcolm Price attended. The man who's set his sights on leading Lewisburg will make education the cornerstone of his Mayoral platform, and will use his success, on and off the basketball court, as an example of what availing oneself of the borough's educational system, and hard work can achieve.

A swell of excitement fills the Borough Office when Malcolm Price enters the Mayoral suite. Jack Cane joins the hubbub in the vestibule and extends his hand, "Damn pleasure, 77."

Malcolm shakes the smiling man's hand, "Mayor."

Cane has Malcolm precede him into the office and points to a chair opposite his desk, "Have a seat."

"I'll stand," the visitor says before realizing there isn't an inch of empty wall space to be had. He leans back against the closed office door and takes it all in.

"Can I get you anything?" Cane asks as he heads to a refreshment tray set on a credenza.

"I'm good, thanks," Malcolm says with the raise of his steady hand, which is in stark contrast to Cane's shaking hand as he pours himself a glass of water. Before he's put the pitcher back on the tray, a fine sweat has formed on Cane's forehead and upper lip, leaving Malcolm to wonder about the state of the Mayor's health – then wonders where the man's thoughts go when he leans back against the credenza. While Malcolm waits for the man to circle back, he tries to square what he knows of Jack Cane with the man who is withering and wetting before his eyes.

Jack Cane is a blonde, tanned, golfer-type, who is approaching sixty, but looks as though he's approaching fifty. Known well as a dandy about town, Jack has had no real purpose in life. When he filed Intent papers in 2017, a repetitive, "No shit," could be heard on borough streets. And when word spread that he was leaving the job well before the end of his first-term, the tongue-wagging usually began with, "well, that didn't take long," and ended with, "the world of work ain't for everyone."

One thing seems certain, the world of work isn't for Jack Cane—never has been—never will be. The Mayor is a man of considerable wealth, all of it inherited by his wife, Monica. Prior to his taking political office, Mr. and Mrs. Cane held celebrity status for no reason other than the age-old real estate adage, 'location, location, location'. Their inherited home sits upon a sprawling parcel of land, once owned by William Penn, founder of the then Province of Pennsylvania.

Cane realizes he's been off in thought, does a little throat clearing, and starts in, "Does this visit mean you are making your run official?"

"It means I'm interested," Malcolm smiles.

"In that case, your opponent, Topher Griffin, has his work cut out for him what with your celebrity status and all. Although…I hear he has Abigail Forrester as his campaign manager. She picks winners—she picked me after all," Cane says while raising his water goblet.

"Not sure Topher still has Abigail," Malcolm smiles.

Jack's hand begins to shake a bit more vigorously, and the fine line of sweat on his brow and upper lip, isn't so fine anymore. "Well…no one has ever accused Abigail of loyalty. A piece of advice, once you enter politics, Malcolm, never give anyone a chance at your back."

275 Market Street

Gretchen and Researcher Randy work for several hours before heading to the game room. She ignores the furtive glances from her assistant—until she's had her fill. "Is there something you'd like to say, Randy?"

"Yes, ma'am. I bet your kid is gonna be a big one."

Gretchen starts a giggle fit and is doubled over in raucous laughter when Malcolm comes in. "Woman, don't laugh that baby out."

Gretchen's laugh turns to tears.

Malcolm pulls her into his arms, "Woman, you're a mess."

She buries her face into his chest, and nods and sobs.

"Pull yourself together. We're going out to eat. Where are you staying tonight, Randy?"

"Philly."

"We'll meet you at the restaurant."

The threesome head to Merchants Square in Colonial Williamsburg for dinner at Si, Pizza. The men share a fried crust pie with white sauce, goat cheese, and roasted chicken, Gretchen picks at a honey chicken taco. Her nibbling here and there bears no reflection on the taco, but rather on the fact that she's experiencing her first bout of baby nausea. The men divvy up the leftovers while Gretchen waits outside. On the way back to Lewisburg, Gretchen takes a call from her father, "Hi, Daddy ..... let me ask ....." she addresses Malcolm, "do you feel like heading to Philly tomorrow?" He nods. "Daddy, we'll see you around three. Say hello to Faye, please."

A disconnect from her phone call coincides with her disconnect from the world. Malcolm spends a very quiet ride home, wakes Gretchen enough to have her participate in the walking to the elevator, and the getting ready for bed routine. He tucks her in, kisses her goodnight, heads to his home office—then back in time…

"Tell me about yourself."

"Nothing interesting about my life, Malcolm. Momma got pregnant at sixteen, Baby Daddy left her before she was showing, she got kicked out of her house and had to scrounge for places to crash until she had me. When she got assistance from the State, she moved us into Tucks where we lived happily ever after." She glanced at the fine black man driving the Mercedes.

He glanced back, "I said tell me about you, Sage."

"Oh, well, in that case my story is so much better. I got the tar beat out of me by girls at school because I was a straight-A student. When I got boobs, I went from girls beating me to boys helping themselves to me. My grades suffered, my attitude hit the shits, and I wanted away from it all. I was ready to bail on life at Tucks when Momma got sick and had to leave her job at the corner mart." **The young woman pulled a shaky breath before continuing.** "I quit school, took Momma's job to put food on the table, and when the money didn't cover her medical needs, I took a job at the escort service, even though she begged me not to. Momma died six weeks ago. Like I said, happily ever after," **she turned away.**

"My damned arrogance got that girl killed," Malcolm angers at himself. He tries to push Sage from his thoughts. He fails…

Malcolm entered the Center ready for Game One of the Semifinals against the Phoenix Suns. He knew Micky Strong was in the stands; he could feel the intensity of the pit bull's stares. The b-baller ignored the dick until his number was announced:

"… and wearing San Antonio Spurs team jersey 77, Theeeee Malcom Price!"

The point guard took center court, tossed a wave to the standing crowd, then narrowed his eyes on Micky. He gave an extra wide smile and swished an imaginary ball in his direction.
The. Crowd. Went. Wild.
Micky got up and stormed from the arena.

~

Sage killed the lights and crouched low at the front door when she heard a vehicle on the pebble driveway—a vehicle that did not have the purr of Malcom's Mercedes. She eyed the security panel over her shoulder just to make sure she remembered to activate it. She had. She turned her head in the direction of footfalls heading her way, held her breath when they landed onto the tiny front porch. Relief flooded at the sound of Malcom's knocked announcement.

"Sage, it's 77."

The terrified woman pulled herself up, unbolted the door, banged the security panel, and stepped back from Malcolm's approaching form.

"Micky knows about the pregnancy," he said as he kicked the door closed behind him.

Sage began to shake, then paced the room. "He won't believe I miscarried, he's gonna think I got rid of it. He's gonna kill me, Malcolm."

The man took hold of his girl's hand, "Get some things, you're staying at the ranch."

"Damned arrogance..." The emotionally tortured man crawls into bed in the wee hours of the morning. His woman feels his presence and curls into his spoon. He holds her and their baby bump until daybreak—a few hours later.

Wish them well, please.

Mick's on the Beach is empty because the beach, Playa Los Cerritos, is empty. Both places are abandoned because it's been raining for the past two days, really raining. The province of Los Santos, where the beach and the bar are located, received about seven inches of rain in the last two days. "The Rains," as they are referred to by locals, don't normally come until October, and when they come Mick closes the tiki-bar for the month. He sends Cloe to the States for a visit with her mother, while he heads to Playa Punta, a fishing beach not too far from the tiki-bar. That's where Micky Strong resurfaces and does his thing—a little fishing, a little drinking, a little gambling, and a little dick-dipping into the local girls. Not necessarily in that order.

For the rest of the year, Mick enjoys his whore Cloe just fine—of course he enjoys her most when she is on the beach sunning and beachcombing, and not cooped up with him inside the tight quarters of the tiki-bar. Cloe Fishbaum is a bit too much for Mick Stone to take. That's why he is busying himself with a little maintenance, a little cleaning, and a lot of ignoring the buxom blonde. It isn't until his whore raises her voice that he is pulled into her orbit,

"Mick! 77 is running for Mayor of some Podunk place in Pennsylvania — or maybe he's running. He hasn't said so yet, but look, his face is everywhere."

A ping of excitement pongs then bangs throughout Mick's body. The *only* smile he's had in two days takes shape and widens. "Let me see that." Mick slides Cloe's tablet across the bar and glares at Malcolm Price. He slides the tablet back, "It says he might run. Let me know when it's official." Mick goes back to his maintenance, his cleaning, and his ignoring. Not necessarily in that order.

Old Estate Road
Every time Gretchen lays eyes on her father's home two things happen—she is taken aback by its beauty, and she is overcome by a trumpeting happiness. The Cottage, where Granger Mitchell resides, is a 10,000 square foot Frank Lloyd Wright designed home. It is a stunning stone structure burrowed into the ten-acre, natural stone and vegetated hillside surrounding it. Aged trees nearly obscure the building, and lush Mountain Laurel bushes run wild on all sides. The interior of the Cottage boasts sundrenched space designed of stone, steel and glass. It is an architectural feat of sophistication and artistry—but mostly, it is Gretchen's childhood home.

Malcolm has barely pulled the Land Rover to a stop, before Gretchen bolts from the car, races to the front door, and commences her shout out, "Daddy we're here." Granger welcomes his daughter into wide arms, and ushers her inside. Malcolm brings up the rear with a wide, warm smile.

As Granger extends his hand in welcome, Malcolm eyes a shiny new wedding band on Granger's other hand. His eyes travel from Granger's face to Gretchen's face. He watches as her eyes travel from Granger's left hand to Faye's left hand. In a single blink of a cornflower blue, reality dawns and sends Gretchen into one of her word mashes. "Oh. My. God. Granger Mitchell has taken himself a bride. Look, Malcolm, matching wedding bands. I know Paris is the city of light and love, but I imagined it a bit bourgeois as a nuptial site for the great Granger Mitchell, but I suppose when the bolt of inspiration hits it hits. I mean, who needs family and friends around for mundane things such as matrimony. After all, wedded bliss is an intimacy that need only be shared by the two entering into such affairs, and..."

Malcolm approaches Gretchen. He takes her face into his hands, "Woman, I'm seeing why these two eloped. Wish them well, please."

Gretchen's eyes latch onto Malcolm's smile, broadens one of her own, and turns to her father and his new bride, "Oh, Daddy, oh, Faye,

I'm sorry. It's just the shock of it all that's caused me to fall short of extending my heartfelt congratulations." The daughter walks to her father and his new bride, and embraces them both.

Four hours later, Malcolm drags his emotionally and physically drained woman to her 3,000 square foot, two bedroom converted Carriage House set back from the main Cottage. He has never stepped foot inside her home, and now there, he is sent back to the first bit of word mash he ever heard from his woman…

Gretchen gasped when the elevator door opened into Malcolm's penthouse apartment. She kicked off her ankle boots. He removed her jacket. She paused at the doorway for a minute taking in the expanse of the space. Then, she began gushing. "This is *beautiful*. The open floor plan is magnificent. I love the exposed brick walls and the heavily treaded wide-plank floors, and the floor to ceiling windows are imposing, almost frighteningly so, and the furniture—it's so classic yet comfortable."

"You sound surprised."

"I am," Gretchen admitted.

"What were you expecting? Black lacquer, chrome and leather?" Malcolm playfully challenged.

"No. No. But I wasn't expecting to see my furniture in your place, either Mr. Price." Gretchen pointed at select pieces of furniture. "That rolled arm, high back sofa with button-tufted cushions, I have it in white, and that mid-century sloped armchair, I have it in green apple, and the distressed wood end tables and sideboard I have them in medium oak. Your color choices are different, but the furniture in this room is an exact match to mine."

Gretchen stopped assessing furniture and studied the man leaning against a brick wall – his legs were crossed at the ankles, his warm caramel-colored eyes were slightly hooded, and his lips had a devilish grin on them. She moved toward him. "Honestly, if you take me to your bedroom and there's a king-sized platform wingback bed with antique silver nail trim, I'll figure I'm in my own bed enjoying another fantasy about you, Mr. Price," she boldly admitted.

"King-sized platform wingback bed with bronze nail trim. And since I'm going to turn your fantasy into a reality, you should call me Malcolm." He pushed off the wall and took one long-legged step forward. He wrapped his arm around Gretchen's back at her waist and pulled her to him. He lifted her against his chest and kissed her long and deep then swung her into his arms and headed to the bed that Gretchen described to perfection. The woman laughed when she saw the man's room. Her laugh faded when he placed her on the bed, his lust bulging hard. Adrenaline pumped through her and she began to shake.

He smiled wide, "I figured you were a tease. You don't do this sort of thing much, do you?"

Gretchen shook her head. "No, but don't go spreading that rumor, I have a reputation to uphold."

"Who are you trying to fool with this supposed reputation, Gretchen?"

"Granger Mitchell, of course. Daddy doesn't think any man is good enough for me, so I let him think I try a few men on for size and toss them into the discard pile. It makes Daddy happy that I agree with him."

Malcolm's smile widened. "I'm sure your daddy is gonna love that you're trying me on for size."

Gretchen laughed. "Yes, well, I've never been with a man like you, Malcolm."

"Black?"

"Bald."

Malcolm laughed big.

Gretchen reads the memory on Malcolm's face, "See, I told you our furniture choice is a perfect match."

Malcolm lifts his woman, just as he did that first night, and growls against her ear, "We're a perfect match. Now, it's time to check out your king-sized platform wingback bed with antique silver nail trim."

Now, what?

After a lovely breakfast with Mr. and Mrs. Mitchell, Malcolm and Gretchen begin their trip back to Lewisburg. Half of the road trip is spent reliving every conversation the four of them had about Granger and Faye's wedding in Paris – Malcolm's and Gretchen's engagement – the magnificent cornflower blue sapphire ring on her finger – Gretchen's tiny baby bump – the adorable moniker, 78, that she gave to their little one – and Malcolm's decision to run for Mayor. The remainder of the road trip is spent with Gretchen digging for information about quiet discussions the men in her life had, to which she was not privy.

"I believe you are about to tell me about your bending of my father's ear," she eyes her man.

"I'm hiring Researcher Randy for six months."

"To do research for the Campaign?" Gretchen asks.

"To do research on the campaign manager," he answers pointedly.

Gretchen swivels in her seat. "Spill."

"When I met with Mayor Cane, he was all twitchy and sweaty, not like a man who is sick, more like a man who is scared. He said if I enter the race, my opponent will have his work cut out for him. Then he readjusted his thinking. He said that since Topher has Abigail Forrester as his campaign manager, I'd be the one with work to do. I suggested that Abigail may no longer be associated with the Topher Griffin Campaign. Mayor Cane said no one has ever accused Abigail of loyalty, and added a piece of advice about never giving anyone a chance at your back."

"Well, Mayor Cane sure put you on notice about Abigail. Now what?" Gretchen asks as she swivels back in her seat.

"Researcher Randy," Malcolm says as he exits I-80.

275 Market Street

Malcolm calls Abigail Forrester to arrange a meeting with her for Monday. Then he places a call to Braun, the architectural firm he used for the penthouse renovation. The answering service puts him directly through to the owner, Stephanie Braun.

"Malcolm, or should I address you as, Mr. Mayor? A bit premature, perhaps, but inevitable," she chuckles. "A pleasant surprise, for sure."

"It's been a while, Stephanie. I'd like to catch up, but I'm pressed for time. I need a very quick job done on the unused space on the top floor of 275."

"What do you need. When do you need it," Stephanie asks even though she will do whatever he needs whenever he needs it done?

"Significant office space, major wiring, and a two-room apartment. Use the rest of the floor space and I need it yesterday."

"You can have it rough, but workable and livable in five days," Stephanie commits.

"Do it. Everyone and everything moves through the back entrance. No work between 9 PM and 7 AM unless it's approved. Thanks, Stephanie." That call is going to cost Malcolm a pretty penny, but the next call is going to be priceless.

Researcher Randy answers the blocked number, expecting **anyone** other than who is on the other end.

"Yo!"

"Kid."

"77?"

"You're working for me for the next six months. Go to the payroll office at Mitchell and Morgan. They are cutting you a check for ten-grand, use it to pay six months' rent and utilities on your current place, pack your stuff and be at 275 by 7 PM." Malcolm disconnects but not before he hears Randy's whoop of excitement.

The hipster dude races out of the privacy elevator and into Malcolm's penthouse at five minutes to seven. He points excitedly at the clock, "Did it. I hit bottleneck traffic the whole way here, but Researcher Randy prevails."

Gretchen laughs. Malcolm groans. "Come on Kid." Malcolm grabs Randy's bags leaving the computer whiz to schlepp his computer wizardry. In minutes, the men join Gretchen in the game room. "Sit," Malcolm says to Randy, "and if you choose the recliner, don't ride it until I'm done."

Randy eyes the plush leather seat, though he sits with Gretchen on the couch, "Temptations are best avoided, you know?" he whispers.

Malcolm hands a piece of paper to Randy, who reads out loud what is written, "Abigail Forrester, Jack Cane, Christopher 'Topher' Griffin." He looks up at Malcolm.

"Do a deep dive on them. Get me everything there is to get. Kid, toe the legal line. Do. Not. Cross. It. If you think an illegal dive is needed, call this number and ask to speak with the Decadent One—speak only to the Decadent One—and don't leave a message about why you are calling."

"Who is the Decadent One?" Randy asks with a raised brow and the pinch and pull of an imaginary handlebar moustache.

Gretchen laughs at the pantomiming villain.

"The Decadent One is with RFI," Malcolm groans a bit. "I'm having second thoughts on this arrangement, and we're five minutes in." While he is grousing, Randy is thinking. Recognition flashes across Randy's face.

"Holy shit, I mean, ah hell, I mean holy shit! The Decadent One is one of the cyber huntresses. Which one? Doesn't really matter which one. The three most famous cyber hackers in the world are women and they work for RFI now. Holy shit, 77, you sure have me playing game in the big leagues."

"Pace yourself, Kid, only take the shots you **know** you can make." Malcolm offers his hand to his woman, and they leave Researcher Randy whooping it up big. On his way out of the game room, Malcolm calls over his shoulder, "The Decadent One is former FBI FICA Agent, Hannah Leavy."

"Damn, 77, she's the Julia Roberts clone."

"Good night, Kid."

"It's sure gonna be, now that I've got the Decadent One on my mind."

Malcolm answers his cell on the way to his bedroom, "You saved me from making a call, Manuel."

"Good to know. Since I did the calling, me first. This is where we're at. Leavy found us enough to work with. Fred, Mike and I will be heading to Texas. Your turn."

"Tell Leavy an employee of mine, a kid named Researcher Randy might call. I'd appreciate her assist. I want to keep the Kid from going too deep."

"Done. I'll be in touch," Manuel disconnects.

Wyldwood, Texas

Sammi Wilcox answers her phone with a wide smile on her face, "Malcolm, it's been too long."

"Far too, Sammi. Is Jason with you?"

"Right here, I'll put you on speaker." In a second, Jason is on. "77, it's good to hear your voice."

"Same. Three investigators from RFI are heading to San Antonio. They're hunting Micky Strong. It's time he pays for Sage. I've offered the ranch for their sleeping and working needs. Have them use the Escalade. And when they ask you two about Sage and me, tell them everything. Everything. We good?"

"We good, Malcolm," they say in unison.

The Women of Texas

Sammi

Sammi and Jason welcome the RFI team to Wyldwood Ranch just before sundown. After the men settle their gear, they join their hosts in an enormous eat-in kitchen. Sammi points to a buffet-style spread of chicken stew, cornbread biscuits, salads: potato and tossed, and pitchers of homebrewed sweet tea and lemonade. While the men eat, she tells them about the girl who was brutally murdered in an idyllic cottage known as Garden Oasis. Hardly polite dinner conversation, but that's why the men are in Texas.

"Sage Finley was a sweet girl who really didn't expect anything from life, she certainly didn't expect Malcolm. She was 19-years old when she died—she'd be in her early thirties now." Sammi shakes her head, "All those lost years." Jason pushes back from the table and opens his arms to Sammi. She moves into them. Without so much as a word, they connect in a deeply personal, and touching way. It's obvious to all that this scene has played out before— many times before. When Sammi is whole again, she continues on, "I didn't think of this at the time, but this is what fills my head when thoughts of Sage push in. If life is measured in terms of endurance, you know, after life kicks you around enough, you get to go off to the happy place in the sky—then there wasn't any way that girl could have survived beyond nineteen.

"Sage Finley was born on the wrong side of happiness to a homeless mother of sixteen who tried to eke out a meager existence. That existence was spent in a housing project where there's very little living and lots of surviving. The way Sage told it, she spent her early years being beaten by girls and her middle years being taken by boys. When her momma got sick, Sage quit school, took a clerk job to put food on the table, and a job as an escort to buy medicine for her momma. On her first night working for Garden of Eve, Micky Strong chose her, then became her regular customer. He banged her around seven ways to Sunday. Towards the end of her momma's life, Sage needed to choose between medicine for her dying mother and her own birth control pills. Her momma got her medicine and Sage got pregnant by Micky. She lost the baby by miscarriage and was just starting to think her life might get onto a better track through the kindness of 77. A little more than three months after Sage Finley met Malcolm Price her life ended the way most people expected it would." Sammi's eyes fill, and her words almost get lost in emotion, "Malcolm's girl and her momma are buried on a tiny hill near a grove of trees here at the ranch. It's the only reason Malcolm still owns this place."

Dinner conversation stopped at that point. Sammi and Jason insisted on handling cleanup by themselves, so the RFI men waited at the table until they were alone. And when they were, the men unleash…

"I've been pissed at Malcolm for holding back information…"

"…and fucking with an investigating…"

"…but he had good reasons for doing it…"

"…like trying to protect Sage…"

"…in life…"

"…and in death."

"We need to get Micky Strong."

Before hitting the sheets, Manuel sets the investigative track for the next day. "Working off the stuff Leavy pulled, we'll start with the former owner of the escort service, Eve Lappier. She uses the same storefront on Stark Street from when she ran Garden of Eve. The place is a little book store now called, Turn the Page."

"No message there. Although it's also a Seger song, one of his best, so who knows," Fred pushes in.

Manuel pushes back, "First, you should listen to Maverick Cross. Second, for someone who makes a damned big deal out of being interrupted, you sure have no problem doing it.

As I was saying, Micky was a regular at Eve's. She probably knows things about the PI, things that didn't seem important a decade ago, or things she's remembered since then, but has kept to herself. Let's push her on him, and on the buxom blonde escort who was sitting in the bleachers with Micky during the last couple of playoff games in 2007. She has a backstory—maybe she has family in the area. If she left San Antonio with the murderer, she's either still with him, left him for greener pastures, or met the same fate as Sage. Maybe Eve will know something. From there we'll head to, Paula's on the Chase, a popular watering hole, big with the sport's crowd. We'll talk with Paula Malone, owner and operator. Maybe we'll get lucky, and find out Stoner hung out there too, and get information on him. From Paula's we'll try to track Chelsea Brady, Stoner's former girlfriend."

Fred jumps in, "If the dominos fall right, we could do that in a day, two tops."

Manuel nods. "Given her line of business, I'm hoping Paula will have some insights into Micky. He was a regular—she'll know some shit about him—the kind of stuff a regular bar patron tells the person pouring the drinks. Maybe she'll hand us a lead on Micky's bookies, or the ID forger. If so, we'll check them out, then hit up the FBI field office, and if we're really crapping out, we'll consider talking to San Antonio PD. I'd rather we keep our investigation close to the vest considering there's got to be some professional angst over this case, and SAPD might want to fuck with us a bit for being in their territory. After all that, we head to McKenna Correctional to press into Stoner." Manuel laughs, "The inmate is **not** going to be happy to see me."

"Who is?" Fred quips.

The RFI men call it a night and start for upstairs. They change course when they see that Jason's set a poker table for five. The men will soon learn they should have gone to bed. Over the course of the next few hours there was a lot of, "folding, checking, raising, and calling," but there was only one who seemed to be enjoying herself.

The losers avoid Sammi's eyes at the breakfast table the next morning; they raise their heads when she addresses them, grunt a, "thanks," when she fills their plates, but none of them looks at her. When Manuel's phone rings, he welcomes the interruption. "What's up, Malcolm?"

"Put me on speaker."

"You're on, what's up?"

"Is everyone in earshot?"

"Yeah."

"Good. I forgot to tell you something. Don't play poker with Sammi, she's unbeatable," he says on a BIG-ASS. LAUGH.

Malcolm hangs up.
Sammi cracks up.
The men pay up.

The RFI team begins their trip from Wyldwood to San Antonio a little before 9 AM. An hour and a half later they arrive at Turn the Page bookstore on Stark Street. They pull into the lot and immediately pull back out after reading the Closed until Monday sign hanging in the store's front window. When they pull to the curb at Paula's on the Chase a few minutes later, they figure they are in for a wait, "Locked up tight," Mike says as he puts the Escalade in park, and hops out.

"It's before 11 AM on a Sunday morning. The place probably didn't close until 2 AM. Let's give it a few minutes," Fred says.

The team is milling around the Escalade when a brand-spanking new white truck comes barrel-assing down Chase Street, screeches around a corner into a narrow alleyway between the bar and a row of small businesses—barely missing the bar and a row of small businesses. The white whiz causes a white light moment for Fred as he jumps out of the way of the truck's front bumper. "Does that truck have a big-ass dent in the hood, and does that big-ass dent look like the letter 'B'?" Fred stammers.

"Don't know. I was looking at the big-ass dent in the front bumper. You must have missed that one when you jumped out of the way," Manuel laughs.

"You mean the bumper that almost took me out?" Fred laughs.

Mike ignores the back and forth, and sprints down the alley. He is alongside the truck when the door swings wide, and a speed-demon exits.

Paula

The woman on the move is in her late forties, is wearing tight Wrangler jeans, a plaid button-down blouse, and a smile that's seen its fair share of use. "Here," she hands off two Brookshire grocery bags, "carry these in. You're waiting on meeee, right?"

"Yes, ma'am," Mike smiles.

"If you're planning on calling me ma'am, you can be on your way. The name's Paula Malone."

Mike smiles wider, "The name's Mike Monopoli."

"Good to know. You bring those bags in for me, Mike Monopoli. I've got a tray of burger patties, and cut fries to get into the walk-in reeefrigeraaator."

Mike peeks inside the Brookshire bags, and laughs out, "Tiny Tina's and…"

"Beef jerky. Tunnnns of beef jerky." Paula laughs BIG at Mike's raised brow. "Had a leeetle run in, or run through at Brookshire's."

Mike eyes the 'B' indentation on the hood of her white truck.

She nods. "Damn 'B' fell off the storefront and landed on my dee-luuxe truck when I was inside apologizing for driving through the joint. Figured while I was there, I'd grab the Tiny Tina's snack cakes and beef jerky from under my front wheeeels. Come on, Mike. I'll put coffee on and you can tell me why you're here."

"Is it okay to bring my partners in?"

"It's not a party 'til there's more than two," she tosses a wink his way.

A few minutes inside the walk-in reefrigeraaator with Paula, and he's walking through the bar, and opening the front door, "Come on, Paula's gonna talk."

Fred points to a package in Mike's hand, "Is that a Tiny Tina's Crunchy Bar?"

Mike smiles and nods.

"Does it have a tire track on it?"

Mike laughs and nods.

"Did white whiz run it over?" Fred laughs.

"Yeah, and a hundred others too."

"Really?" Manuel chimes in, "Are there any cupcakes, I could go for something cream filled."

"Or brownies?" Fred pushes in. "Nothing like a brownie with a cup of coffee."

Paula arrives right on cue with a pot of coffee, and an apron full of treats. She sets the men up, tosses the RFI business card Mike gave her onto the table, and does a round of introductions. "I read about you guys after you busted up The Realm. Pretty impressive, sheehhtt." she drawls. "Mike said you're here about Micky Strong. I hope you bust him up, reeeel good. What he did to that sweet girl is beyond criminal." Paula shakes her head as though she's trying to shake an image free.

Fred has a hunch and plays it. "Any chance you saw pictures of the crime scene?"

"Lord save us all, I did. Saw the whole disgusting lot of them right there at the bar ….. and right over there," Paula points to an area by an old jukebox, "is where I puked my guts up."

Fred commiserates a bit, "Almost lost it myself when I saw them. Who showed you the pictures?"

"Micky's nephew, Stoner Strong. I kicked his ass out and told him to never come back again. Sick twisted little bastard."

"When was this?"

"Around the time Stoner went up for hacking. He said he needed someone to help Micky out with something. He showed me the pictures, I puked my guts up, and told him I wouldn't help Micky out of a burning building. In fact, I said, I'd set the damn building up in flames and lock him inside." She adds pensively, "Then

I set about making amends to the good Lord. Are you a praying man, Fred?"

A smile takes hold of the affable detective's face, "The last time I prayed was when Mike was on his deathbed. Look where that got me, Paula," he laughs BIG.

A smile takes hold of Paula's face, "Looks like you're right with the Lord. Good for you Fred, and good for you Mike."

Fred takes a bite of his brownie and sips some coffee before turning back to the disgusting topic at hand. "Did Stoner say what kind of help he was looking for? You know, to help Micky out?"

"Nope, but he took the pictures from an envelope that had Malcolm Price's name and what I assumed was his address in Lewisburg written on it. I think the sick bastard wanted someone to send those pictures to 77."

"Any idea why Micky would want 77 to get pictures of the murdered girl?"

"I don't know anything for sure, but during the NBA playoffs in 2007, Micky came in one night spewing about his call girl leaving him for Price. I thought he was full of sheehhtt, but then the girl ended up dead, Stoner ended up with pictures of her body hacked to Hell and back, and there was an envelope with Malcolm Price's name on it. Don't take you three detectives to figure it out."

Fred shakes his head. "Nope it don't. Just one more thing, Paula, what month was Stoner in with the pictures?"

She doesn't even have to think about the question, "July. That's when I had to have the carpet over by the jukebox replaced."

The team hangs at the bar while Paula fixes them, "The best damned burger and homestyle fries, you'll ever eat." They confirmed her brag by eating Every. Damn. Bite. When Fred gets off his stool to leave, Paula starts rummaging through an enormous slouch-bag she pulls from beneath the bar. "Hang on a second, Fred." She reaches in, and one by one she places baggies full of singles, and small bills onto the polished oak top. Next comes a wrinkled, dog-eared People magazine. "Brad and Angie are on the skids. Who saw that coming?" she laughs. Next, out of the bag is a fistful of banded utility bills. She slaps them onto the bar, and pulls one free. She takes the statement from inside, and writes a phone number on the back of the envelope. "I own Paula's on the Chase, and Malone's on the Bend. If you need more information, it'd be easier to call my house than trying to track me down. Keep it in your shoe, Fred, I only give that number out to friends."

After crapping out on Chelsea Brady, the men do some sightseeing in San Antonio then head back to Wyldwood for the night.

Eve

The former brothel owner is getting a late start back to San Antonio from a weekend trip to Austin. Still, she manages to pull her Saab in front of Turn the Page bookstore at five minutes to nine. She opens her little place, turns on the lights, puts on a pot of coffee, puts out fresh bowls of potpourri chips, and fluffs the pillows on several reading chairs. Two of her regular customers are in the store by ten browsing the shelves. If history repeats, and repeats, and repeats, these two will spend close to an hour roaming the aisles. They will choose a book they're both interested in reading, they will flip a coin to determine who will read it first, the winner will pay for the book, read it, share it, then own it when the sharing is done.

Today, the pair selects *Bullet Bungalow,* a cozy mystery written by new author Kitt Mahoney that's receiving great buzz and making a pretty penny in online sales. Unbeknownst to the two women heading out of Turn the Page, they walk through a door being held for them by Kitt Mahoney's partner, Fred Serpico.

"Thank you," they titter.

"My pleasure, ladies," he smiles *that* Fred Serpico smile.

"Wow," one says when Fred heads inside.

"Damn," says the other. "Do you want to go back in. Pretend to look for something?"

"I'm not that good at pretending. He'll know I'm ogling."

The women are still hashing it out when Manuel Xavier and Mike Monopoli walk past.

"Morning, ladies."

"It sure the hell is," one says as she begins following them back inside. Her forward momentum is halted by her friend, "Come on. We're making a spectacle of ourselves."

"Haven't started removing my clothes, yet."

"True, but you've unbuttoned your shirt down to your girls."

"Have I?.....Well, I'll be damned."

The women titter away.

When the last of the RFI men push into the bookstore, Eve prepares herself for a hug from the long arm of the law. She goes to the door and locks it. "I'm out of the business, gentlemen, so whatever this is about, make it fast."

Eve Lappier does not look like someone who owned an escort service—she does look like someone who owns a bookstore. She is a slight woman, maybe 5'4" tall, has a slender frame, short cropped brown hair, and brown eyes. She hasn't a lick of makeup on and her clothes scream "suburban soccer mom"—khaki pants, a blue polo shirt with a little bookmark logo on the breast pocket, and running shoes. If Leavy hadn't provided the intel on Eve Lappier, the men would think they were in the wrong place.

Fred Serpico takes point on the meeting and hands Eve a business card, he waits until she reads it.

"RFI? The team that broke The Realm?"

"That's right, Ms. Lappier," Fred smiles wide.

Eve chuckles, "I barely know how to use my purchase and sales software on my computer, so you guys might be in the wrong place if you're looking for a cyber hacker."

Fred chuckles right along with Eve, "This is about Micky Strong."

Eve stops chuckling right quick, "No good murdering bastard, I hope you guys bust him and bury him."

"Who do you think he killed?" Fred asks.

"Sage Finley and maybe Cloe Fishbaum."

"Who is Cloe Fishbaum?"

"One of my girls, one of my former girls. Micky replaced Sage with Cloe. He paid for her services during the tail end of the Spurs run for the Title in 2007. Cloe disappeared around the same time as Micky. She's either with him or she's dead. My money's on dead."

Fred shoots a quick look at Mike who excuses himself to make a call to Leavy.

Fred points to two chairs, "May we sit?" He quickly assesses the woman who nods and moves toward the chairs. *She's caught between forward and reverse. On the one hand she wants us out of her respectable business, on the other hand she still has work to do from her former life, namely, taking care of her girls.*

Eve breaks into Fred's thoughts, "What Micky Strong did to that kid keeps me up at night. Knowing I had a hand in what happened to Sage cuts me deep, I'm sorry, that was a horrible choice of words. This is a really difficult topic of conversation, and I'm bound to put my foot in. I hope you'll accept that I carry pain and guilt about Sage, every day, so if I start talking about me and what I lost because of Micky, I know it's nothing compared to what Sage lost." Eve makes sure Fred registers the depth of her sincerity.

He nods.

"I started out with a legitimate dating service, I couldn't make ends meet and I was going to close shop. A few of the girls I'd sent out on dates, real dates, convinced me to offer a whole new line of dating experience. Sort of for shits and giggles, I put together a list of services the girls would provide, places where the girls could be taken, and rules of engagement; basically a contract for how far a customer could go. Some men like to hit, some women like to be hit. And some women, like me, allowed that shit to happen." She gives Fred the chance to say his piece, one way or the other. He doesn't, so she continues.

"The girls who came to work at the Garden chose what they were comfortable doing and having done to them, and the guys chose what girl they wanted to do it with. Sometimes, the price point was the deciding factor for what package a guy would choose, but when it comes to men and sex, money isn't the only driving force, if you get what I mean."

Fred nods.

"Micky became a regular at Garden of Eve from Day One. He chose the premium package every time—a beautiful young woman who he could rough up a little, but who looked good on his arm. He liked having people think he got the girls on his own, then he'd get pissed because everyone knew he had to pay for a girl— but he kept paying. When Sage started working for me, Micky latched on to her, made her *his* girl. He paid me big to keep her from going out on other calls. She never knew Micky owned her." Eve drops her head and gently shakes it from side to side. "I didn't think he'd kill her," she says as tears fill her eyes.

Fred waits until she pulls herself together.

"The last time I talked to Sage was when I set her up with Micky for a Spurs playoff game. Sometime that night I got a voicemail from her saying she was quitting the business. The next day Micky started calling every hour on the hour asking for another date with Sage. I told him she was out of the business. When he finally accepted that I was telling the truth, he flipped his shit. He started demanding I tell him where she was and who she was with. I couldn't tell him anything because I didn't **know** anything. Then he started raging that 77 took Sage from him. I thought he was nuts. A couple weeks went by with no calls from Micky, then he was back during the Finals looking for a replacement. He chose Cloe Fishbaum. After the series, I never heard from Cloe again. She didn't call to quit like Sage did, she just disappeared. I heard rumors from my other girls that Cloe took off with Micky, but I can't say for sure.

"As soon as I heard about Sage's murder I knew Micky did it. Cops from Wyldwood and San Antonio started digging into Sage's life, and it wasn't long before they ended up here. I told them I thought Micky Strong killed Sage Finley. I kept the whole Malcolm Price part of the story to myself, figuring if there was any truth that 77 took Sage from Micky, the investigators would figure it out. Anyway, the cops became regulars in my place, not paying regulars mind you. I think they were hanging around hoping Micky would come in for another girl, or something. Needless to say, my customers didn't like rubbing elbows with law enforcement, so my customers stopped coming around. I closed Garden of Eve within a couple of months of Sage's death and opened Turn the Page, mostly on a whim to use the space I'd already leased. Truth, I'm gonna have to close shop if sales don't pick up."

Fred looks around the place, "Too bad. This is a nice place."

"Thanks," her response wistful.

"Any idea where Micky and Cloe might have gone?"

"No clue. I didn't know Micky other than him being a customer ..... wait a second, the intake form ..... I'm sorry, I just remembered that my customers had to fill out an intake form when they first came in for a date. It was a stupid thing, sort of an administrative thing I did from when I ran a legitimate dating service. Hold on." Eve scurries through the bookstore, weaving effortlessly around display racks, and reading nooks. She pushes through a back door, and comes back many minutes later waving an 8.5 x 11 piece of blue paper with writing on both sides.

"Micky Strong's intake form. I forgot I had it until just now. You can take it if you want."

Fred nods. "What's on the pink paper?"

"That's Sage Finley's intake form."

"Any chance I could have that too?"

"Sure, but the only thing written on it is **Tucks** for her residence, and in the section asking why she wanted to work at Garden of Eve she wrote, **so Momma doesn't die.**"

"Well, shit."

Eve scoffs, "That's what I said when I found it out back."

On the way out of Turn the Page, Fred purchases a copy of *Bullet Bungalow*. The bookstore owner sighs, "Such a good read. Your woman will love it."

"My woman?" Fred asks.

"Excuse me for saying, but that book doesn't seem like something you'd be interested in," she shrugs.

Fred laughs big, "I'm interested, believe me, I'm interested." He leans in and lowers his voice, "My woman wrote this."

"Kitt Mahoney is…"

Fred's smile is so wide it looks positively painful. He takes one of Eve's business cards from a little holder by the cash register and pockets it. "I'll have Ms. Mahoney sign it for you. Take care, Eve."

"You too, Detective. And thanks for stopping by Turn the Page."

When Fred and Manuel join Mike in the Escalade, he has information to share, "Leavy got stuff on Cloe Fishbaum. We're heading to her last known address."

Gladys

Cloe Fishbaum last lived with her mother, Gladys, in a tiny house in Port San Antonio, a redeveloped area at the site of the former Kelly Air Force Base. Like most everyone else in Port San Antonio, Gladys Fishbaum works for one of the private-sector employers that support the military and commercial aircraft industries. Gladys eyes the Escalade parked in front of her little house as she pulls onto a gravel driveway. The men exit their vehicle, and are immediately greeted with, "If she's dead, I don't want to know."

Fred approaches the anxious woman, "Ms. Fishbaum, my name is Fred Serpico, I'm with RFI." Fred hands Gladys his business card. She takes a quick look, shield's her eyes from a bright sun in a near-cloudless sky.

"You the guys that busted up The Realm?"

Fred nods.

"Ah, shit, what's Cloe got herself into now?" Gladys takes a couple steps toward her house. "Well, come on. Let's get this over with." The space in the tiny living room sucks in around the three larger-than-life gorgeous men standing elbow to elbow in the tiny fishbowl-sized Fishbaum home, "Come on let's go to the patio," Gladys says over her shoulder. "I have to say, you guys are in the right line of business, I'm about to tell you whatever you want to know in – r.e.a.l. s.l.o.w. m.o.t.i.o.n – just to keep you around. You sure are some fine-looking men. Your women must be something else to keep you three happy."

Fred smiles wide, his long dimples cut his face and his eyes spring to life, "Personally speaking, ma'am, my woman is most definitely something else."

Gladys points at Fred, "I like you, come on and sit."

Fred gets right to the point, "We're here about Micky Strong."

Gladys nods, "I hoped as much. There are only two things I know about Micky; he supposedly killed that sweet girl up in Wyldwood, and my daughter's been with him a dozen years and she ain't dead. Unless that's why you're here, to tell me she's dead. If it is, I don't want to know."

Fred shakes his head. "We don't know anything about Cloe, ma'am, but we'd sure like to know about her," he smiles.

"Cloe's a good kid, or I should say she's a good woman, she's thirty-four now. She came home one day and said she and Micky were heading out of town for a while. It's been a long while, more than ten years. I don't know where they are, but she comes home every October and spends the month. I guess it's the rainy season where she lives, so Micky closes their business, he goes his way and she comes here. They might be living in Mexico because she always comes home with a tan, you know the kind you get at a beach, and she throws a lot of Spanish words around. She doesn't speak the language, but she throws out fiesta or siesta, that sort of thing."

"Ms. Fishbaum, do you have any pictures of Cloe?"

"Sure, come on inside." Gladys turns to Mike and Manuel. "You two stay put, it's too tight inside for all of us. Besides, I like him."

Mike and Manuel laugh, "Yes, ma'am—his woman likes him, too," Mike calls after her.

"I bet she does," Gladys calls over her shoulder.

Cloe's mother grabs a photo album from a shelf under the coffee table and hands it to Fred. "It's old fashioned, I know, but I take pictures when she's here, then print them and keep them in there." Gladys points to several pictures, "Those are from Cloe's trip home last October."

Fred smiles wide when he sees the word Playa written across the buxom blonde's cropped tee. He pulls his cell from his pocket, "May I?" Gladys nods and allows Fred to take pictures of the paper printed pictures in her old-fashioned photo album.

Sage

On the way back to the ranch, the team takes a spur of the moment turn off the main thoroughfare in Wyldwood. They go in search of a fairytale cottage turned gruesome murder scene. There is no such cottage to be found. At the end of a pebbled pathway, and for as far as the eye can see, there is a massive, well-tended field of flowers. The men get out of their vehicle without comment, and walk the field in silence. The space offers the visitors a bounty of beauty, and the opportunity for quiet reflection. There are stone benches to sit upon, birdbaths full of feathered friends, and wishing wells perfect for a toss of a penny or two. Scattered about the beautiful space are wood arbors with creeping floral vines, wrought-iron gliders for two, garden gnomes and tree sprite statutes peeking from around trees here and there. When the men have had their fill and head back through the gated area they notice the sign.

Garden Oasis
In Loving Memory Of
Sage Finley

The sign is nearly overgrown by abundant bushes and bushes of yellow Carolina Jessamine and Blue Evening Primrose.

What about Panama?

It's been two and half days since the construction team hired by Stephanie Braun began work at 275. Malcolm and Gretchen spend most of their time away from the building and Researcher Randy spends most of his time in the guest suite keystroking and earbudding. He is doing both when a touch on his shoulder nearly sends him to the ceiling.

"I'm sorry, I didn't mean to startle you, I have a meeting with Malcolm Price. I guess I'm a few minutes early." The unexpected redheaded visitor extends her hand, "I'm Abigail Forrester, Mr. Price's campaign manager."

Randy closes his laptop and stands to greet her, "77 is out, he'll be back at 11 for a meeting, you must be his meeting."

Abigail nods and smiles, "Must be, and you are?"

"At the moment, I are wondering how you got in?" Randy eyes her suspiciously.

"I came up through the back, with the construction workers. Are they building campaign space?"

Randy is spared the question and answer session when Malcolm appears out of nowhere. "Abigail, come with me."

As they leave, Randy closes and locks the door behind them, but not before he hears the first of Malcolm's words. "The construction on this floor is for campaign space which will be done in the next few days. Anyone who works on the campaign will be required to use the back entrance. There's ample parking in the back of the building. No campaign work before 7 AM and no work after 9 PM, unless approved by me."

Abigail nods, "And Randy, who is he?"

"A researcher I hired."

Abigail pauses. "I usually do the hiring for campaigns, Malcolm. I've been working in the field for years and have a crew of carefully vetted professionals."

"Use them where you want them. Randy stays and he reports to me."

Abigail nods and takes a seat opposite her new boss and begins outlining her schedule and plans. "For the next two weeks, I'll be devoting my time to the August 1st announcement. I have a list of venues that we should discuss."

"Hufnagle Park," Malcolm says.

"For what?"

"The announcement. It will be made at Hufnagle Park."

Abigail slumps a bit in her seat. "You can't be serious."

"Abigail, I am always serious – and rarely flexible. I will seek your expertise when I need it. Assess whether you can work within those confines. Now, if you will excuse me, I have another meeting." Malcolm stands and waits for Abigail to follow his lead.

The Lone Star State

The RFI team spends the morning at the ranch reviewing the information they received from Paula Malone, Eve Lappier, and Gladys Fishbaum. An outline of Micky Strong is taking shape and the men start extrapolating information from their interviews to help shade in that outline.

Fred starts things off with the clap of his hands. "The intake form from Eve Lappier confirms what we already knew about Micky Strong, age, address, employment. The only piece of information we didn't have before is that Micky is fluent in Spanish – which fits nicely with the information we got from Gladys Fishbaum about Cloe throwing around some Spanish words here and there." Fred stops and pulls his ringing cell from his pocket, "Serpico," he answers.

"Fred, it's Paula. When I talked with you the other day, I was focused on what Micky did to Sage. I was thinking later, I should have focused on what Micky likes to do, it might help you."

"Anything you can provide will help. What does Micky like to do?"

Paula offers a snort of derision. "He's religious about his booze, his bets, and his broads. Aside from those three things, Micky would drone on about the Spurs, deep water fishing, and engineering marvels, you know like the Great Wall of China, or the Hoover Dam. He was always talking about some tall-ass bridge in Southeast Asia, or some islands in the Middle East made out of palm trees or some sheehhtt. I don't know, but Micky knows a ton about that kinda stuff, it's really the only interesting thing that ever came out of the bastard's mouth."

"I appreciate the call, and you never know, Paula, this information could crack the case."

Before hanging up, the woman who knows how to get a customer and keep one coming back adds, "You guys have time, stop in before you head wherever your heading, first round's on me."

"Will do, thanks Paula."

Fred shares the information with Manuel and Mike. The RFI grounds manager, who shares Micky's interest in tall-ass bridges and palm tree islands, hops onto the internet, "The bridge could be the Langkawi Sky Bridge in Malaysia, and the islands in the Middle East are probably the Palm Islands in Dubai," Mike informs.

Fred gets up from the table and stands in front of a wall of windows for a bit of Serpico processing. He starts his roll with a clap of his hands. "Okay, Micky Strong is 42-years old when he goes on the lam. He's a private dick, so he knows what it takes to go off the grid. He's flush with money from betting big on 77. He loves boozing, betting, and broads; the Spurs, deep water fishing, and engineering marvels; he speaks fluent Spanish. He brought a woman along for this new life, so he's most likely going to find a place to take root. The woman who's with him comes home every October during rainy season. She's all nice and tanned and throws Spanish words out like candy. In several photographs, this woman is wearing a cropped T-shirt with the word Playa on it."

Mike, who is still searching the internet says, "What about Panama."

"What about Panama?" Fred and Manuel unison him.

"It's a Spanish-speaking country, geographically way south of Texas, the height of its rainy season is October, it's surrounded by deep fishing waters, the beaches are called Playas, and it has the damn Panama Canal."

Fred and Manuel smile and repeat Mike's earlier question, adding a little excitement. "What **about** Panama."

Fred smacks Mike on the shoulder, "This feels right."

Mike growls, "That's my bad shoulder."

"Shit. I keep forgetting." He smacks Mike again on the other side.

"Shit. I was kidding. **That's** my bad shoulder. Jesus, Fred. Stop hitting me on the shoulder."

Manuel ignores the hijinks and places a call to Leavy. "Feel like diving, today?"

"How deep am I going?"

"Deep enough, oh, Decadent One. Mike has a hunch Micky is in Panama."

"Oh, because Stoner made a trip there?" she asks.

"What the fuck trip did Stoner make to Panama?" Manuel snaps, as he puts his cell on speaker.

"The trip that's highlighted on the travel shit you wanted me to get on Stoner Strong. Jeez, Manuel, you guys need to start reading the shit I get for you."

"Do you want to yell at me a bit, Leavy?"

"Damn straight."

"Yell at me later. Tell me about the trip Stoner made to Panama."

Fred and Mike are on their feet, cross-cutting one another as they pace the room. They stop and focus on Leavy's words.

"Stoner flew into Tocumen airport and then to Los Santos Augusto Vergara airport in early 2009. He returned to San Antonio three weeks later," Leavy informs.

"Remind me to kiss you when I get back," Manuel enthuses.

"I'd rather you read the shit I give you, Manuel." Leavy disconnects on a laugh.

Manuel makes a call to Special Agent in Charge, Dean Freeman, at the FBI field office in San Antonio requesting help arranging a prison meeting. The RFI team will be heading to McKenna Correctional Facility to meet with Stoner Strong on Monday, July 22nd, the first available date.

With some time on their hands the men throw in with Jason — they saddle up and work the ranch for the next few days. Yeehaw!

Deep in the Heart of Texas

McKenna Correctional is a minimum-maximum security facility in Waco, Texas, that houses 5,700 inmates in two separate wings. The middle section of the facility is known as the Center — it is used by inmates from both wings, for enrichment programs, and dining. As a hacker-for-hire, Stoner Strong is housed in the minimum security wing and would stay in that wing every minute of every day if he could. He cannot. All inmates are required to attend programs offered in the Center which means that Stoner, and other minimum security inmates, spend upwards of four hours a day rubbing elbows with the maximum security inmates. So, when Wendell "Stoner" Strong is told there's someone waiting on him in a meeting room, he jumps at the opportunity to get out of the Center. The prisoner changes his mind pretty quick when he sees who his visitor is – Manuel Xavier, the man who Stoner blames for his current housing predicament.

"What the fuck do you want? You have three minutes," Stoner snaps.

"Well, in that case, let me cut to the chase. First-degree murder charges are being filed against Micky Strong in the death of Sage Finley."

Stoner shifts in his seat, "You found Micky?"

"Nope," Manuel stretches his legs in front of him and crosses them at the ankles.

"So, you've got no one to stick the charges to. I'm done," Stoner nods to the guard.

"I'm gonna stick the charges to you Wendell," Manuel says with a shit-eating grin running ear to ear.

The inmate shakes his head to the guard who stops moving toward him.

"You can't get me for first-degree shit. I didn't have anything to do with Sage Finley's death."

"Wrong. I've got you cold for accessory before the fact on a first-degree murder charge. You provided the intel to Micky so he'd know when Malcolm Price was away and Sage Finley would be alone." Manuel pauses, then he pushes. "Someone is going down for Sage Finley, it's either you or Micky."

Stoner shifts uncomfortably in his seat. "Let's hear what you got."

Manuel smiles wide. "You hacked Malcolm Price twice in 2007. Once for background information—once for reconnaissance information. I don't give a shit how Micky used the background stuff, but the reconnaissance stuff gave Micky everything he needed to know — and what he needed to know was when he could get to Sage Finley. I can almost hear your report to Micky – Price is leaving Texas on August 1st. He's going to Lewisburg for a celebration. He'll be back on the 5th."

Stoner shifts a bit more.

Manuel laughs, "Looks like you'll be relocating to the maximum security wing of this fine institution – just as soon as you are tried and convicted of accessory **before** the fact."

Stoner bristles at the named charges, but sets his bravado. "Old news, Manuel."

The seasoned interrogator swiftly changes subjects. He pokes the bear. "Hey, I heard Chelsea Brady left your ass."

"Leave her out of this," Stoner growls.

"Can't. She's the one who's helping us get you," Manuel smirks.

Stoner snorts a laugh. "She can't, she won't."

"She can, she did. Ms. Brady gave us the key to the storage unit. I heard she was mighty pissed about your piece of ass on the side. Should have kept your woman happy, Stoner. There's a saying, Happy woman, happy life. In your case it's probably gonna be, Unhappy woman, you're doing life."

"Fuck you, Xavier."

"This is how I'm gonna fuck you, Wendell. We found lots of stuff in the storage unit. It leads from Micky straight to you."

Stoner's face twitches. He **knows** this conversation is going way off the rails.

Manuel smiles even bigger. "Now that we have the pictures of the murder scene, taken by the killer, and linked to you, we have you cold on accessory **after** the fact. Let's recap. Before the fact. After the fact. And that's a fact."

"What do you want?" Stoner snarls.

"Same thing I've always wanted, Micky Strong."

Stoner leans forward against the table. "I don't know where Micky is, so now what?"

"We charge him with first-degree murder in absentia. He's put on trial, which means you are put on trial, and you go down for the shit show."

"Or?"

"Depends."

"On?"

"How long it takes you to give up Micky." Manuel sits quiet for several minutes.

"Screw you, Manuel. If you had shit on me, you'd be filing charges." Stoner nods to the guard.

As the inmate begins walking away Manuel lobs his final shot, "We know Micky is in Panama. It might take us some time to track him down, but when we do, we'll get him on first-degree murder, and we'll get you on before and after."

On the way back to Wyldwood, the RFI team members place wagers on how long it will take Stoner to break. Given the ass-whooping they received from Sammi Wilcox at the poker table, the wager from these three losers seems a bit bold.

The frizzball.

As soon as the last nail was gunned into the apartment behind the campaign office, Researcher Randy moved out of the guest suite and into his new digs. He's still working in the guest suite, located just on the other side of his boss' office. That. Is. Way. Too. Close. For. Comfort. The researcher is ten minutes late for a meeting when…"Kid. You have ten seconds to get in here."

Randy rounds the corner.

Malcolm directs, "Sit."

"I'll stand—it makes for an easier getaway."

"Start with the worst," Malcolm directs.

"That's a jump ball, 77, they all have issues. I'll start with Abigail Forrester because I do not like her. Biggest issue, besides her frizzball hair, is that she might have a personal relationship with Benton Brettenvue." Randy hands Malcolm dozens of pictures of Abigail and Benton at various events taken over the years.

Malcolm flips through, "Is there more?"

Randy hands him another set of pictures, "I took these last night."

The boss flips through the set. The angering boss growls, "Kid."

"It's research. The Decadent One suggested it; she's the bomb by the way," Randy breaks into a wide smile.

Malcolm follows suit. "Yeah, she's the bomb. Explain the pictures."

"There are pictures of Abigail and Benton everywhere – on the internet, in gossip rags, and credible news outlets. The pictures look innocent enough, you know, movers and shakers at the places where movers and shakers congregate. But I couldn't bust the feeling that there is something else between the two, so I scoured every damn thing ever written on Abigail Forrester. I found an article on her success rate at picking the right candidate to work for—it was sort of a 'chicken-egg' thing. Does Abigail have a knack for picking a winning candidate—or does Abigail make her candidates winners. Anyway, there are 7 words in a thousand-word article that connect the evil forces – Benton Brettenvue helped launch Abigail Forrester's career."

Malcolm nods.

"So, I've got pictures of the two of them, a sentence about the two of them, and a hanky feeling about the two of them, but I'm not sure how to move forward, so I called the Decadent One. She dove deep and found out that when Benton Brettenvue was being investigated by the FBI about his association with Antonio Alvarez, Abigail Forrester was called in for an interview by the Feds. Leavy thinks the FBI talked to Abigail because she was at some meet and greet with the Peruvian crime lord at the Brettenvue estate. Strange elbows rubbing together, you know?

"So, Leavy directed me away from that historical mess and said I should focus on what's happening between Benton and Abigail now. That's why I followed Abigail to Philly, waited in my car with an expensive new camera, and took pictures of Benton Brettenvue letting himself into Abigail's condo. He's got keys, security codes, the works. I was still waiting when he left six hours later."

Malcolm smiles wide, "Good job, Kid. Don't do it again. Tell me what else you have."

"Mayor Jack Cane, isn't sick, at least there's nothing in his medical records that says he's sick. It's anyone's guess why he's jumping the Mayoral ship, but there's no guessing about the current state of things between him and the frizzball. There are tons of pictures of the two of them at some event or another over the past couple years. Most of them are happy, happy pictures. About six months ago not so happy, happy pictures start surfacing. Before you know it, Mayor Cane is calling it quits, and in steps Christopher 'Topher' Griffin. As for your opponent in this Mayoral hat-tossing competition, there's nothing all that objectionable on him other than he is a big proponent of energy production through fucking fracking. He's been working alongside the spear headers on getting fracking into Pennsylvania in a measurably big way. For every group opposing fracking based on environmental, political, or financial reasons, Topher has been writing counter-opinions that are used by every group proposing fracking. He has made a name for himself in the lobbying circuit and has put his money into the coffers of – when fracking takes hold, we will be rich."

Randy pauses. Malcolm waits. Randy gets to the crux of the matter. "I have a lot of questions about the frizzball, 77, but this is **the** ultimate headscratcher. Why did Abigail want to work for you?"

Malcolm waits for the Kid to work the question.

"The frizzball **manages** her candidates – there ain't no managing gonna be happening with you .... although she did manage to get into your lair." Randy takes a quick look over one shoulder, then over the other before continuing. "We'd better be on guard because the red devil – **Is In The House!**" he repeats the call that 77 made at every meet and greet in San Antonio.

"Keep digging," Malcolm says with a shake of his head. He leaves that meeting and heads to the Campaign office, knocks on Abigail's office doorframe since there isn't yet a door, "Have minute?"

"Always," she chirps.

"Tell me about the announcement."

Abigail gets up from her seat. "On July 28[th,] a teaser will be sent out letting the Press and the community know you are going to announce on August 1st. That information is circulating already, and garnering a lot of local excitement, but a formal announcement will get huge national press. That morning, a news crew will follow you to the Borough Office at 11 AM and film you while you file your Intent papers. There'll be a photo op with Mayor Jack Cane after which a select group of reporters will ask questions. After that, the official announcement is scheduled at Hufnagle Park at noon, followed by a family celebration at the Park."

"I'll answer two questions."

"Even if the questions are about Sage Finley?" Abigail throws a metaphorical boulder into the waters expecting a huge splash – she gets nearly a ripple.

Malcolm nods and leaves. On his way back into his living space, he locks the door behind him and steps into the guest suite "Kid, keep the penthouse door locked at all times."

Randy gives a thumbs up, a mumbled, "Damned red devil," and goes back to keystroking.

Malcolm finds Gretchen in the game room reading a legal document. "You going back to work, Woman?"

"Just the opposite. This is my letter of resignation."

"Yeah? Am I your meal ticket, now?" Malcolm smiles.

"Nope. You're my employer." Gretchen smiles devilishly.

"I'm liking the sounds of this," Malcolm joins her on the couch and pulls her onto his very hard lap. "Woman, it's been a while."

Gretchen straddles wide and teases her man. "I'm going to make you a proposition and when you accept, I think we should seal the deal in the shower."

"A proposition? I'm listening."

"Make me your campaign manager."

Malcolm brushes Gretchen's hair from her face looks deeply into her eyes and ups the ante, "I have a counter-proposal."

"I'm listening."

"Make me your husband."

Gretchen starts to move off his excitement, he holds her tight knowing there's a word mash coming. "You're announcing in a week, Malcolm. Is a wedding even possible? I mean there are so many things to do when you're planning a wedding, even a small wedding, marriage licenses, music and flowers, oh, Malcolm there has to be flowers, and you need a suit, what am I saying, you have a thousand suits, but I'll need a dress, oh a dress, do you suppose I'll be able to find something appropriately beautiful, and..."

"Woman, you're breathing for two, take a breath."

Gretchen looks into her man's eyes. "You must have thought about this, Malcolm, any ideas?" she asks ever so hopeful that he has ideas and they can get married before the Mayoral announcement.

"I have," Malcolm nods, "Granger must know someone who can marry us. We go to the Cottage have a family only ceremony and gathering. It can be done." The very serious man takes the hopeful woman's face in his hands and locks eyes. "Gretchen, I want our wedding to be about us, we're inching closer to a time when that will be impossible. Let's do this for us." He places one of his gigantic hands onto her expanding bump, "For the three of us."

Gretchen wraps her arms around her man and kisses long and deep. "Rain check on the shower, I have a wedding to plan. I need to call Faye!" she squeals as she runs to their bedroom.

Malcolm calls after her, "You do the flowers; I'll do the music. I don't want to hear your feminist anthem on my wedding day saying I don't own your ass, when I most surely do, Woman." Malcolm laughs big when Gretchen retorts, "Yeah, yeah, you own my ass Malcolm, and I own yours, too."

"Yes, Gretchen, you do," he whispers.

Matrimony and machinations.

The morning begins before sunrise when Gretchen receives a call from the RFI Compound. "Gretchen, it's Maura. I know it's early, but I wanted to tell you that the Budding Ones arrived this morning. Steve and I are the beaming parents of two perfectly healthy and beautiful children. Our son, Noah Kenzi, was born first weighing 6 pounds 6 ounces, followed by his sister, Cordelia Claire weighing 5 pounds 5 ounces."

"Oh, Maura, what wonderful news. Please give our best to Steve, and we look forward to meeting the Budding Ones."

"One last thing, Gretchen. Good luck pushing 77's kid out." Maura and Gretchen wail in laughter.

The soon-to-be bride and groom hit the shower. "The next time we're here, you'll be my husband," Gretchen squeals and does a happy little two-step.

"Let next time wait, Woman. Pay attention." He spends long, loving minutes kissing her, tracing every inch of her with his fingertips. When she's breathless and near boneless, he sits on the built-in seat, and pulls her onto him. He rests one of his hands on her tiny baby bump, "Woman, I didn't think I'd ever find you, so I didn't bother looking. I'm damn glad you came to me in need of a favor."

Gretchen giggles. "If you don't mind, Mr. Price, could you speed up the foreplay? I find myself in desperate need of another favor?"

He eases into his woman, and favors her gently to an intense orgasm.

Philadelphia

Abigail has been up all night mapping out a plan to force Malcolm Price out of the Mayoral race. She knows his undoing is Sage Finley. That is why Abigail enlisted the help of Penny Meehan, a former tabloid reporter who somehow landed a gig at Liberty Rings, a century-old, reputable Central Pennsylvania newspaper. Luckily for Abigail, Penny hasn't left her nose for trashy news behind—which is why the two of them are digging deep on Sage Finley. It is also why Penny will be one of two reporters called on at the Press push after Malcolm Price files his Intent papers.

After several quiet minutes at her computer, Penny offers, "There's not much on Price and Finley. Seems weird that there's so little information. I mean he was HUGE and she was a HOOKER, a dead hooker, at that. I can't tell if the snooping shelves are bare because no one in the industry tried to get the shit, or if they were blocked from getting it, or paid off not to get it, or if everything has been scrubbed, but something is off."

"Which means?"

"That there is a story here, and I'm gonna find the fucker."

275

Malcolm finds Researcher Randy in the guest suite a little before 8 AM "You're up early."

Randy smiles. "Gotta get the goods on the frizzy redhead. So, is this a social call, or is there something I can do for you, 77?"

"Do you own a suit?"

"Sports coat and slacks, why?"

Malcolm tosses Randy a black silk tie, "We're going somewhere later, look nice, wear that tie, and be ready to leave at noon."

Randy is ready at noon—not exactly how Malcolm hoped he'd be ready—but close enough. The kid's slacks and sports coat are black, his T-shirt is new, white and ironed, his Vans slip-ons are black with white rubber soles, and the tie Malcolm gave him is looped around his neck and knotted in a classic Windsor.

The impeccably dressed Malcolm is the anti-Randy. He is wearing a black virgin wool, classic fit Brioni suit, with crisp white Stefano Rici, barrel-cuff dress shirt, a black silk Bironi tie, and black, textured, Armani loafers. He takes one more look at the hipster, shakes his head, and moves to the elevator, a mumbled, "Still gonna marry the woman even though he's part of the package. Come on Kid, we gotta get Mama Girl."

Old Estate Road

Gretchen left 275 Market Street that morning a single woman—when she returns she will be married to the man who has become her everything. Before she steps foot from Magnetite Black, she thrills at the bushes and bushes of Mountain Laurel in full white puffy display all along the estate property. She loves the Pennsylvania state flower, particularly loves that it blossoms late at the deeply wooded Cottage on Old Estate, and that is in full bloom on her wedding day. Gretchen grabs her cell phone from the passenger seat and takes a picture, "Just beautiful, and a perfect beginning to this day." Her excitement builds when she steps inside the stone, steel and glass estate, and sees the preparations Faye has made. The brand new Mrs. Mitchell takes hold of Gretchen's trembling hand.

"The ceremony space is set in the solarium and is awash with sunlight right now, but by 4 PM the lighting will be filtered and soft," Faye explains.

Gretchen's gasp at the beautiful room lets Faye know she is more than pleased by the stepmother's efforts and vision, "Oh, Faye, this is simply the most beautiful thing I've ever seen."

The solarium has been emptied of its overstuffed comfy furniture and replaced by flower draped, black wrought-iron fencing, set at an angle to create an aisle for Gretchen and Granger to walk. At the end of that aisle is an altar of black wrought-iron candelabras of varying heights. The room is awash with bright natural light boldly highlighting shiny back urns of all shapes and sizes overflowing with every imaginable white flower, Iceberg roses, snow hydrangea, daisies, jasmine, Queen Anne's Lace, and flowered Yucca vines.

Many minutes pass before Gretchen speaks, "Faye, it's like I've fallen into a beautiful fairytale."

Faye takes Gretchen's hands. "I believe the day you and Malcolm found one another you did fall into a beautiful fairytale."

The soon-to-be-bride's eyes brim with tears as she pulls Faye toward her, "I believe you are right."

After another stroll through the room, Gretchen is shooed off by Faye. "Go get ready, call me if you need help with your dress," the stepmother-wedding planner says with the wave of her cell phone.

Gretchen does a little two-step of excitement then races through the house, a gleeful whoop following her up a wide center stairway. She stops at the entrance to the room where she grew up; amazed that it has been emptied of childhood mementos and filled with vases of white roses, and white satin and lacy things. She runs her fingertips across a beautiful white satin robe hanging from a beautiful white satin hanger, hanging next to her beautiful white wedding gown. Upon her vanity is a lovely garter with Gretchen's and Malcolm's names embroidered on the satin, and next to the garter is a black velvet box with a note from her father.

> *Dear Gretchen,*
>
> *On a wedding day in 1986, a bride entered her dressing room and found this box waiting for her. That bride honored me by wearing what's inside as she walked the aisle and stood beside me to exchange marriage vows. I hope you will honor me and the memory of your mother by continuing that tradition.*
>
> *I am sure when Malcolm sees you walking toward him, he will be filled with the depth of love I had for your mother on our wedding day. I know in my heart and soul that Mrs. Delaney Rae Hamilton Mitchell is with us today. Knowing that pleases me, so.*
> *Love, Daddy*

Gretchen opens the black velvet box and finds an exquisite pair of platinum set, oval cut, diamond drop earrings. She closes the box and goes to the window that overlooks her Carriage House, the one her mother once loved. She places her hand onto her baby bump and whispers, "I have the perfect name for you – if you are a girl, of course. Don't tell anyone, but I'm thinking that Mrs. Delaney Rae Hamilton Mitchell will have a granddaughter come the New Year."

The father of the bride.

At ten minutes to four a knock comes upon the bride's door. She opens it and finds Granger Mitchell, the larger-than-life man who loved and raised her, coming now to give her to another. The father-of-the bride, is resplendent in a black suit, crisp white shirt, and black tie.

Gretchen runs her hand down the beautiful silk, "It's lovely. It's just like Malcolm's," she says with a wide smile.

"He asked that I wear it. It's quite nice. I may just spruce up my tie collection."

Gretchen giggles, "Daddy, customarily a tie collection consists of a variety of colors and prints, your 'collection' consists of a number of the identical tie, a navy-blue silk."

The beaming father steps full into his daughter's bridal room, "It's time. Perhaps you should take off the satin robe."

Gretchen smiles. "I was just touching up my makeup. You know, Daddy, I went to a wedding once where the bride decided a final sweep of her garishly inappropriate red lipstick was needed before she walked the aisle. Well, the bride dropped the lipstick tube, and watched in horror as it bounced down the front of her dress leaving garish red splotches here, there, and everywhere. Thus, my satin robe covering is staying on until the last minute."

Granger approaches his daughter, "You're nervous, you tend to sputter on when you're nervous." He places his hands onto her shoulders, "May I."

Gretchen nods as her father removes her robe—beams at his expression when he sees her in her wedding gown.

"Oh, Gretchen, you are lovely."

The bride twirls, then stops to inspect her final wedding ensemble in a full-length mirror. She is thrilled with the bohemian, hippie-chic, white two-piece gown she chose. The top piece is an off-the-shoulder, antique lace top with attached elbow length lace sleeves. The bottom piece is a banded skirt of soft satin that brushes the floor, and hides all signs of her baby bump. She's teased her hair slightly at the crown and pulled it into a sleek ponytail, and went soft and dewy with her makeup. The only jewelry she wears are her mother's wedding earrings, and her gorgeous cornflower blue engagement ring which she has moved to her right hand.

Gretchen pulls herself from her reflection and grabs a box from her vanity. "Oh, Daddy, look." She takes Malcolm's wedding ring out of a sleek black box and hands it to her father.

Granger inspects the brushed platinum, east-west black onyx ring, letting out an admiring whistle, "Cartier, a pretty penny was spent here."

"Yes. Well. The ring didn't cost as much as the courier service to get it here in time, but I suppose he's worth it." Gretchen slides the ring onto her thumb.

Granger nods, "Yes, he is worth it, and he's waiting for you, Gretchen." The father extends his hand, and leads his daughter to the man who has taken top billing in her life. Halfway down the stairs, she asks, "The Justice of the Peace has arrived, right?"

Granger smiles wide, "The Senior Justice of the Pennsylvania Supreme Court, Samuel Stanton, has arrived. He has agreed to perform the wedding of the next Mayor of Lewisburg, Malcolm Price, and the woman who has captured his heart."

Gretchen Rae Mitchell
&
Malcolm Price
request the honor of your presence
as they exchange vows of marriage.

Granger escorts Gretchen into the solarium, pauses at the end of the aisle, kisses her cheek, and steps to the side. Gretchen turns confused eyes to her father, then turns her eyes to Malcolm who is standing alone at the end of the tiny aisle. Her heart skips a beat—starts again—then speeds up until it is beating thunderously in anticipation at what happens next.

Malcolm takes a step toward her and stops. A string quartet begins the first notes of, *When a Man Loves a Woman*. Malcolm waits until the song is nearly done then walks to Gretchen, "You are lovely, give me a minute, please." Malcolm Price steps off to the side toward the father-of-the-bride. "Mr. Mitchell, I never formally and properly asked for your daughter's hand in marriage. Sir, I love your daughter beyond measure. I ask that you consent to Gretchen becoming my wife?"

Granger slaps Malcolm on the shoulder with one hand and shakes his other, "Better late than never, son. You have my blessing."

The groom steps to the bride and offers her his hand, "Will you do me the favor of marrying me?" he winks.

"I will."

The intended couple walk hand in hand, and stand before Supreme Court Justice Stanton, who does his thing then steps aside to let the bride and groom marry one another.

"Gretchen, the moment I saw you I knew I would take a knee one day and ask you to be my wife. You have undone me in every possible way, forever." Malcolm slides a simple platinum wedding band onto Gretchen's finger.

Gretchen admires the ring and smiles wide at her man, "Malcolm, my forever started when you said my name for the very first time. You have undone me in every possible way, forever." Gretchen slides the black onyx wedding band onto Malcolm's finger.

When they are pronounced husband and wife, Malcolm takes his bride's face into his hands and whispers what he said when he proposed, "I want you more than I need you, and I need you more than anything in this world." The husband kisses his wife.

After a lovely celebration, Malcolm walks Mama Girl to the Land Rover for her return trip with Researcher Randy, "You've been awfully quiet."

Mama Girl places her hand to her son's face, "I've been remembering a young me thinking I might have love and marriage one day. Truth, son, it's better seeing you have it." The mother pats her son's face, "Go find your wife and unwind a bit."

They embrace big.

He addresses Randy, "Make sure you walk Mama Girl in."

"Pish, 77, Mama Girl is spending the night at 275 with me."

Mama Girl laughs big. "The young man said he'd take me deep. Truth son, I haven't a clue what this white boy says half the time."

Malcolm laughs big, "You're doing half better than me, Mama Girl."

Get that mutha fucker!

Manuel, Fred, and Mike board the RFI Learjet at Halifax Stanfield International Airport with a destination of Waco Regional Airport having spent nearly a week at The Compound waiting for Stoner to see the light. Special Agent in Charge, Dean Freeman, at the FBI field office in San Antonio called Manuel to say that the inmate is ready to talk and a meeting was scheduled for Monday, at 11 AM. Freeman's call came at 7 AM Sunday morning, making Fred Serpico the winner of the bet. He won nothing more than bragging rights, which he uses—all the way to Waco.

Central America
The rains have stopped, the beach is full, and Mick Stone's whore is sunning herself on a canvas lounger, her shaded eyes glued to her iPad. A flash of movement from the beach catches Mick's eye—the flash is his whore running toward him, boobs bouncing, hands waving, and mouth mouthing, "He's in the race; 77 is in the race, and he's got a woman who might be having his kid. There's a picture of her with her hand on her belly. That means there's a kid in there."

Mick grabs the iPad from a breathless Cloe, reads the headline, watches the news reel, and exclaims, "Hot damn, Cloe, Mick's heading home. I've got a new set of pictures to take."

"What?"

"Just an expression—like saying you're going to see a man about a horse, but you're really going to take a piss."

Cloe giggles, "Is that what that means?"

Mick shakes his head and takes hold of Cloe's hand, "Come on. Let's celebrate. Everyone drink up, Mick's on the Beach is closing early."

McKenna Correctional Facility

Stoner isn't even seated when he starts looking for assurances from Manuel, "What can you do for me, man?"

Manuel stretches his legs long, picks away imaginary lint from his jeans, and smiles wide, "Depends on what you do for me, man."

"I'll tell you where you can find Micky and what his long game is."

Manuel pushes himself up, heads into the hall, and calls FICA Director, Stacy Remington. Ten minutes later, he's ready to deal with Stoner.

"This is the deal, a once in a lifetime, sweet deal." He pauses and trenches *that* smile of his. "You help us find Micky Strong – we file first degree murder charges and a shitload of others against him. You testify against him on everything and we don't file the before and after accessory charges against you. You'll be seeing some additional time for U.S. Postal violations for sending the pictures, and for the Malcolm Price hacking we never charged you with."

"How much time?"

"Three years."

"Too much time, Manuel."

Manuel pauses, then asks a question he damned well knows the answer to, "Do you have access to a computer in this place?"

Stoner laughs. "I'm a hacker, I don't have access to shit in here."

"I can get you a computer and internet access as part of the deal."

"Can you keep me from having to go to the Center?"

Manuel eyes the prison guard who's standing at the door.

"You could probably get it cut by half."

"Done," Stoner says as he slams his hand onto the table.

Manuel turns back to the guard, "Any lawyers around?"

The guard nods, "I'll get one. If the prisoner moves a muscle, you have my permission to kill him."

The deal is signed, sealed, and given to Special Agent Freeman.

Manuel takes a seat opposite Stoner, "Time to give up Micky."

Stoner does not even pause. "He changed his name to Mick Stone. He and his whore, Cloe Fishsomethingorother live on Los Santos Province in Panama. He owns Mick's on the Beach, a little tiki-bar at Playa Los Cerritos. If he's not at the bar he's fishing at Playa Punta Lobos."

Manuel nods and Mike heads out into the hall to make a call.

"Leavy, it's Mike."

"You've got something?"

"Yup, and I need something."

"Am I diving?"

"Yup. Do a deep dive on Mick Stone, that's the new ID on Micky Strong. He's living in Panama on Los Santos Province, and owns a tiki-bar named, Mick's on the Beach, at Playa Los Cerritos. Get what you can and send it along."

"Will do. Anything else?"

"Transfer me to Rocco."

"Ah, Master Michael, the pleasures are mine."

"We have a lead on Micky Strong. He's living as Mick Stone in Panama. We need a flight plan into Los Santos Augusto Vergara airport."

"Si. Good fortunes on your hunting."

Mike is back in the meeting room in time to hear Stoner explain Micky Strong's long game.

"Micky's gonna hack to shit any woman Malcolm Price gets serious about and if she's pregnant when he does it, he'll be orgasmic."

A single name bangs around inside the RFI team members heads.

Gretchen

Playa Los Cerritos
Mick's on the Beach is closed by the time the RFI team arrives. Manuel places a call to Malcolm.

"Manuel, news, I hope."

"Fred, Mike and I are in Los Santos Panama. Micky Strong lives here as Mick Stone, owner of a tiki-bar called Mick's on the Beach at Playa Los Cerritos. The place is closed for the night, but first thing tomorrow we hope to have him in custody."

"Manuel, I will consider his capture a wonderful wedding gift."

"You got married?" Manuel snaps.

"Is that a problem?" There's dead air. Malcolm fills it, "Talk to me, Manuel."

"Micky Strong has a long game. According to Stoner Strong, and I quote here, 'Micky's gonna hack to shit any woman Malcolm Price gets serious about and if she's pregnant when he does it, he'll be orgasmic.'"

"Manuel, get that mutha fucka!"

Where did he go?

Cloe Fishbaum is clearly working beyond her skill set. Through fits of starts and stops, the bikini-clad babe struggles mightily with the mundane tasks of opening the tiki-bar. Shutters and awnings, padlocks, and patio furniture set her dithering. Mike walks over and offers his services. "Having a bit of trouble?" he smiles.

Cloe shrugs, "I never should have agreed to take care of the place."

Mike reaches out and takes the set of keys, "Here let me." He unlocks the tiki-bar, folds back the shutters and rolls out the awnings. "Here," he says as he hands Cloe the keys. He waits until she enters the bar, then steps inside after her, "Where's Micky?"

Cloe smiles, "You know Micky?" Her smile fades when Manuel and Fred join them inside.

Manuel hands Cloe a business card, "We're with RFI, independent contractors working for the FBI. We're here to take Micky Strong aka Mick Stone into custody."

Cloe scans the space for a way out of the tiki-bar. There isn't one.

"Ms. Fishbaum, we're prepared to take you into custody, as well," Manuel informs her.

"For what?" Cloe starts to panic.

"Aiding and abetting a suspected killer." Manuel explains.

"Micky didn't kill that girl," Cloe stammers.

Manuel pulls the pictures of the murder scene and tosses them onto the bar, "That girl? Sage Finley? Yes, Ms. Fishbaum, Micky most definitely killed that girl, and he took pictures of that girl, and he sends a yearly set of those pictures to Malcolm Price as an anniversary gift."

The buxom blonde bimbo glances at the pictures and starts pulling deep racking sobs, "Micky's gone. He left yesterday."

"Where did he go?" Manuel barely holds his rage.

"He said he was heading home to take a new set of pictures." Cloe's face blanches when she looks at the pictures of Sage, again.

"Where was he heading?" Manuel demands.

"Wherever 77 is. He hates the man."

Manuel calls the local authorities. When they arrive he tells them, in perfect Spanish, that Ms. Cloe Fishbaum needs to be held until United States authorities sort out what charges will be filed against her. Then he and the other RFI team members hightail it to the airport. On the way, Manuel calls Malcolm Price.

"Manuel...?"

"Micky's on his way to Lewisburg. We're on our way back, but we're hours behind him. You shouldn't expect us until well after midnight. You need to keep Gretchen locked down, and

Malcolm, Micky's woman said he's heading home to take a new set of pictures."

Malcolm storms out of his office. He finds Gretchen perched on the sofa looking at wedding pictures on her cell phone. She turns her brightly lit smiling face to her man and immediately loses the smile, "Malcolm, what's wrong?"

"Where's Randy?"

The Kid enters the room from behind Malcom and Gretchen, "I'm bringing up the rear, 77." Randy stops talking when he sees the look on Malcolm's face.

Malcolm points to the space behind Randy. "Are there people in the campaign office?"

"A couple of girls doing some mailings."

"Get them out, follow them downstairs, and lock every damn door on your way back up."

Randy sprints from the room.

Gretchen starts to get up, "Gretchen, stay where you are."

"Malcolm, what on earth is going on?"

"Woman."

Randy shoots Gretchen a 'what's up' look when he returns and receives a shrug of her shoulders.

"Micky Strong is heading to Lewisburg," Malcolm lets that sink in.

Randy fills the silence, "Micky Strong, the dude who killed Sage Finley?"

Gretchen's head swings practically from her shoulders, "You know about Sage Finley," she asks mystified.

"I'm Researcher Randy, of course I know about her. I know every damned thing about 77."

"How long have you known," Malcolm asks.

"I knew the rumors for years, then when Gretchen asked me to research you when you worked at LewPen I learned more, though there's not much on the internet, and when I saw Sage's name on Abigail's computer the other day, I went diving again..."

Gretchen swivels toward Malcolm. "Abigail is researching Sage. Why?"

"My guess is she wants me out of the race and she's working from within. She probably wants a pliable mayor like Topher Griffin in office. I don't know what her end game is, and right now I don't give a damn. We have way bigger problems than Abigail Forrester."

"Micky Strong," Gretchen and Randy say in unison.

"He goes by Mick Stone, now. He's on his way from Panama where he's been living ever since he murdered Sage. The RFI team can't back get here until midnight. Manuel said Micky is well ahead of them and might already be in Lewisburg." Malcolm takes his cell from his pocket. He pushes one button and is immediately connected to Captain Damian

Johnson, "Jet, Micky Strong is heading to Lewisburg."

"Brother, I'm on injured duty from your last shit show. Bring Gretchen to the house, you can fill me in, and we'll make a plan."

Surprise of a lifetime.

      Micky Strong is in Malcolm Price's orbit, and he is flush with purpose. He leisurely walks through Hufnagle Park, finds a bench that gives him a perfect view of 275 Market Street, places a plastic bag onto the bench and pats the contents inside. "A ham and swiss on Rye, a can of soda, and a 13-inch box that holds a brand new 12-inch blade. What more could a man want? A gun," he answers with the pat at the waistband of his jeans. "Yup, I'm good to go."
Micky grabs his bag and sprints across the street when the underground parking garage door lifts. He walks a few steps away from the brick building when a black Land Rover pulls out. The killer of Sage Finley, the hopeful killer of Gretchen Mitchell, turns in time to get his first glimpse of 77 and his platinum blonde woman. As they head down Market Street, he sprints under the garage door before it closes tight. Several hours later, the Land Rover returns. Within minutes, Mr. and Mrs. Price have parked and have keyed in an access code to the privacy elevator. Micky has what he needs – he keys in the code, "The elevator comes back down empty, or the end game takes place in the garage." The elevator comes back empty. Micky hops inside, shuts the door behind him, takes a

seat, and waits. "Next time you call for your steel box, you'll get the surprise of a lifetime, Mr. Malcolm Price."

Shut up, Micky!

The husband and wife are flat on their backs, on their bed, holding hands. They have been alternating between staring at the darkened ceiling, and watching the minutes tick away on the digital clock that sits inches away. Malcolm's cell vibrates shortly after midnight startling Gretchen who quickly covers her rapidly beating heart with her trembling hand. "It's Randy," Malcolm whispers to his wife, "What?"

"I hear noises coming from the staircase, maybe from the landing between the apartment and the campaign office. I think we have company."

Malcolm and Gretchen are on their feet and moving, "Damian was putting officers around the building, and in the alley. Maybe they moved inside. Stay on the phone, and do not leave the campaign office," Malcolm directs. The man on the move tucks one of his handguns into the waistband of his jeans, takes the other in his hand. He motions for Gretchen to follow him to the elevator, and bangs the call button, "Did you bring your cell?"

"Yes."

"When you get in, call Damian and ask if his men moved inside."

The elevator announces its arrival at the penthouse with a ping. Malcolm kisses Gretchen's head, "Get in and lock it down."

As the door begins sliding open, Gretchen yelps in surprise, and grabs hold of Malcolm's arm. He swings her as far behind his back as possible, "Micky," he growls at the man stepping off the elevator.

Both men raise and point handguns— Micky's is pointed at Gretchen. The glint of a butcher's knife in Micky's other hand catches the terrified woman's eye.

"That's for you honey," Micky snarls.

"Get the fuck out of my home," Malcolm demands.

A demonic laugh is Micky's first response, followed very quickly with, "Not until I take your bitch and baby, like you took mine."

Randy grabs his laptop and starts keying an IM to the Decadent One. He gets an immediate response…

> **Randy: 9-1-1.**
> **Leavy: Explain.**
> **Randy: Tap into security cameras at 275 Market Street, 8th floor. Get an ID on who is on the top floor landing.**
> **Leavy: That's the RFI team.**
> **Randy: Gotta go.**

Randy cracks open the campaign office door. Three men point three very big-ass guns at him. He shuts the door, and whispers, "The Decadent One said you're RFI."

"Get out here," Manuel whispers. Randy steps into the hall. The men do the universal finger to the lips thing, "Tell me what's going on," Manuel whispers.

"I heard noises out here, and called Malcolm. We weren't sure if it was the cops that Captain Johnson put around the building, or if it was Micky Strong."

"The cops are still outside," Manuel informs. "What was Malcolm's plan if Micky showed up?"

"He was going to get Gretchen into the elevator and lock it down."

"If Micky's in there, he came up the elevator. That probably means they are all in the living room."

Manuel and Fred know the layout of the penthouse, and quickly explain it to Mike, "On the other side of this door, there's a hallway that leads to a game room, that leads to a hallway, that leads to an open floor living room. There's no chance that we can get in and surprise Micky."

Randy interrupts, "You can get to the kitchen through my apartment. There's a door now."

"What?"

"Courtesy of new construction. Come on."

Fred stops the men's forward movement. "We need a diversion."

Manuel and Mike nod.

"I need a key fob and security code for the parking garage,"

Manuel hands off his set of keys and the code.

Fred tells his team, "Get in place at the kitchen door. I'm going to the garage and call for the elevator. When it starts making its descent from the penthouse, that should cause Micky some concern. That's when you should make your move. I'll jump into action as soon as the elevator makes it back to the penthouse. I'll need a minute to get in place." Fred moves quickly down the stairs and out the alleyway door.

"Looks like we're at a standstill, 77. Your bitch can't get all the way behind you, what with her being blocked by that chair, and that baby bulge bulging and all. I guess that means I have a perfect shot at that Charlize what's-her-name knockoff you're banging. You sure do attract beautiful women, 77." Micky keeps his eyes on the man he hates most in the world, but addresses Gretchen, "Did he ever tell you how gorgeous Sage was."

"Shut up, Micky," Malcolm demands.

Micky laughs, "No, he didn't tell you. 77's not the kind to boast about his women. Let me do it for him. Sage was tall, about your height. She had hair the color of coal, that went all the way to her ass—she had a great ass—she was a great piece of ass, wasn't she 77."

"Shut the fuck up, Micky."

"She had beautiful green eyes, and lips— well, her lips were perfect for…" Micky shuts up at the sound of the elevator coming to life behind him.

Malcolm takes advantage of the split-second break in Micky's concentration. He swings full around and grabs Gretchen, just as a shot rings out. She falls to the floor, scrambling for cover behind the chair. She watches Malcolm swing his arm back toward Micky, who is banging back toward the elevator, seemingly unaware of the bullet wound to his bicep.

"MICKY STRONG! DROP THE GUN!" Manuel yells. "DROP THE FUCKING GUN, MICKY!"

The enraged man tries to raise his gun hand toward Malcolm, realizes that he's wounded and can't move his arm. "It's your fault Sage is dead," Micky screams.

Malcolm raises his gun and points it at the man he hates most in the world.

The degenerate laughs, "Go ahead, 77. Shoot me!" He laughs again, "Look at that. The b-baller CAN'T MAKE THE SHOT!"

Malcolm takes a step toward the bleeding man, "You fucking killed a helpless woman." Rage fills him, almost takes him, almost breaks him.

"MALCOLM PRICE! DROP YOUR WEAPON!" Manuel yells.

The ping of the arriving elevator breaks the moment. Malcolm lowers his weapon, and his head. Fred steps from the elevator behind Mikey, puts his gun to the criminal's back, and takes the knife he's still holding tight in his hand. "Micky Strong, you are under arrest for the murder of Sage Finley, and a whole bunch of other shit."

Intent Papers

The arrest of Micky Strong is kept quiet so Malcolm Price can file his Intent papers and formally announce his candidacy without all that mess tarnishing the day. He is dressed and waiting in the campaign office for Abigail Forrester to arrive. Gretchen and Researcher Randy are hiding in his new apartment listening in.

"Abigail."

"Good morning, Mr. Soon-to-be-Mayoral-Candidate."

Malcolm smiles, "Some things happened last night of which you are unaware, Abigail. I believe they will affect your plans. Micky Strong was arrested and is being held on charges in the murder of Sage Finley. So the dirt you've been trying to dig up on me, to force me from this race, is gone. Your leverage is gone." Malcolm pauses a minute before continuing. "I will be filing Intent papers, and I will be running for Mayor. I will also be making a statement on August 5th – the anniversary of the murder of Sage Finley, a beautiful young woman, who I loved once upon a time. I will be telling our story, and answering for my shortcomings. You are fired. You will not be saying a single word about Sage between now and my statement. If you do,

I will put every penny I have into finding out why you want me out of Pennsylvania politics."

Abigail looks as though she is about to speak.

Malcolm speaks instead, "Get out."

Malcolm Price has his wife and mother by his side as he files his Intent papers, and on stage at the announcement at Hufnagle Park. The crowd of more than two thousand goes wild when 77 introduces his new wife, and announces the impending birth of 78.

The only person in the crowd not celebrating is Abigail Forrester. She makes eye contact with the Mayoral candidate; waits for his attention to be pulled away, before issuing a quiet threat. "I may not have Sage Finley to use against you, but there's something in your past that I can use to bring you to your knees." Abigail takes one more surveying look at the stage.

"The mother. Let's take a peek-see into her past."

The End

More to come …

Please enjoy the teaser for my next book in the series,
Torment…

TORMENT

THE MANAGER

--- PULLING THREADS ---

Book Ten

SHERYLL O'BRIEN

Tower of Power

Abigail Forrester is pissed. She has been in a raging mood since August 1st. That's the day Malcolm Price fired her from his Mayoral campaign. For more than a month now, his parting words have banged a torturous beat in her head…

"Some things happened last night of which you are unaware, Abigail. I believe they will affect your plans. Micky Strong was arrested and is being held on charges in the murder of Sage Finley. So the dirt you've been trying to dig up on me, to force me from this race, is gone. Your leverage is gone." **Malcolm paused a minute before continuing.** "I will be filing Intent papers, and I will be running for Mayor. I will also be making a statement on August 5th – the anniversary of the murder of Sage Finley, a beautiful young woman, who I loved once upon a time. I will be telling our story, and answering for my shortcomings. You are fired. You will not be saying a single word about Sage between now and my statement. If you do, I will put every penny I have into finding out why you want me out of Pennsylvania politics."

Abigail looked as though she was about to speak.

Malcolm spoke instead, "Get out."

The seething woman picks up a wooden block from her desk, turns it over and reads the written name on the bottom. "Malcolm Price," she hisses as she moves the block from one hand to the other and back again. "**You** were supposed to be my newest block, Mr. Price, an important part of my Tower of Power – not the most important playing piece, but…" The woman admires the impressively tall tower of wooden blocks set in the center of her desk. Takes a minute to remind herself of the investment she's made in its construction. "I have painstakingly plotted and planned, maneuvered and manipulated, played and laid most every man who is represented by a block on that tower." She lifts one of the rectangular pieces and reads the etched name on the bottom, "Benton Brettenvue." Abigail laughs, then sneers, "**You** are terrible in so many ways, Benton, particularly between the sheets, but you've been mostly useful in helping me inch toward my ultimate goal – though you almost fucked me royally with that whole Antonio Alverez debacle…"

"I don't like coming here, Benton."
"Don't worry, Celia is out of town."
"I don't give a rat's ass about your wife. It's the fucking FBI knocking on your door **and** my door that freaks me out. Next time you want to introduce me to some international crime lord, don't."

Benton scoffed, "There isn't going to be a next time. Antonio Alvarez is behind bars—Cappa Escobar is dead—The Realm is disbanded—and Dominique is serving a life-sentence. The FBI hasn't been able to prove my involvement with any of the shit that's gone down. I am free and clear, and so are you."

"What about Roland Gaffney?"

"What about him," Benton stopped his roaming and stared at Abigail.

She stared back. "The former Director of FICA is sitting in a Federal prison on charges of treason because of his association with The Realm. I'm sure he's expecting help from someone — that means there **is** someone — someone powerful enough to make sure Gaffney doesn't sing."

"Don't know – don't want to know, Abigail."

"Don't bother with the bullshit, Benton. You know you're up to your ass in **it** and **it** has everything to do with The Realm."

Abigail places Benton's block back onto the tower, "You almost dragged my ass into that fucking shit show. Won't happen again – the next time the Feds come knocking on my door, they'll be getting the goods on you, Benton." She goes back to the other block in her hand, "Malcolm Price," she runs her fingers over the blonde woodgrain, "You may have put up a roadblock, you may have forced me to take an alternate route, but you will not keep me from reaching my destination, Mr. Price."

Abigail handles the block a bit more then places it into a desk drawer. She wants to slam that drawer closed, but rather, she inches it shut. "No sense in bringing down the whole damned tower because Malcolm Price bested me. This time."

From a television located one floor below her office, there comes a thunderous roar. A studio audience is showing its unrestrained enthusiasm when they hear Malcolm Price has arrived at WNEP for an interview on *Sunday PA*. Abigail drains the last few sips of a way-too-early Kahlua sombrero, and takes one more mental review of that August morning, the one that has temporarily detoured her course…

Malcolm Price had his wife and mother by his side as he filed his Intent papers at the Borough Office, and on stage at the announcement at Hufnagle Park. The crowd of more than two thousand went wild when 77 introduced his new wife and announced the impending birth of 78.

The only person in the crowd not celebrating was Abigail Forrester. She made eye contact with the Mayoral candidate; waited for his attention to be pulled away before issuing a quiet threat. "I may not have Sage Finley to use against you, but there's something in your past that will bring you to your knees." Abigail takes one more surveying look at the stage.

"The mother. Let's take a peek-see into her past."

ABOUT THE AUTHOR

She is not dead.

Sheryll O'Brien crafts characters without constraints. She tells them who they are, then let's them show her better versions of themselves. She gives them life and they live it beyond her wildest dreams.

Sheryll is a lifelong resident of Worcester, Massachusetts, where she is wife to the most supportive husband ever, and mother of two adult daughters, one who refuses to leave her home and the other who refuses to tell her where she lives. Of most significance, she is MammyGrams to the sweetest six-year-old, Hadley.

Sheryll worked several years in the fundraising community of Worcester County, writing grants for non-profit organizations. She began writing for her own pleasure after surviving brain surgery and breast cancer. Happily, for her fanbase of family and friends-—she is not dead.

If you have enjoyed reading my book, I would very much appreciate you taking a few minutes to write a review and post that review on amazon.com and goodreads.com.

The opinion of readers can help prospective readers make a purchasing decision.

To learn more, please visit my website, www.pullingthreadsnovella.com subscribe to my blog for updates on future projects.

I would absolutely love to hear from my readers, you can email me at,

pullingthreadsnovella@gmail.com